Breaking Through the Waves

Breaking Through the Waves

Book Two of the Hawaiian Crush Series

E. L. Todd

Sydney rubbed the sleep from her eyes. "Are you cooking everything in the house?"

Coen smiled at her as he placed the plates on the table. "No. You didn't have anything so I had to go to the store."

She got closer and looked at the pancakes, eggs, and bacon that littered the table. "Are we having company?"

"No. But you need to eat."

"Everything?"

"You lost weight. I can tell. You're going to eat."

"I love eating. That isn't a problem."

"Well, then your metabolism went haywire."

"I was just depressed," she said sadly.

He pulled out the chair for her and made her sit down. She did as he commanded and plopped down, scooting her chair in. After the hot sun woke them up that morning, they went back to bed in her room. When she woke up, he was gone.

"I didn't realize you knew how to cook," she said as she ate her eggs.

"There are a lot of things you don't know about me."

"Like what?"

He chewed his food for a moment before he spoke. "I can write upside down and backwards."

She raised an eyebrow. "Are you left handed?"

"Yep."

"That's interesting. It explains why you're good with your hands."

He laughed. "That's just from practice."

"Tell me about your family."

"My dad is in construction. He's built a lot of hotels along the coast. My mom is a housewife. I have one brother who goes to the university as well."

"What's he like?"

"Dumb as shit."

"Well, you are related," she teased.

He smiled but didn't retaliate. "What about you?"

"I have a mom."

"That's it?"

"Yep."

"So your mom never remarried?"

This conversation was taking a turn in the direction she didn't want it to take. "Uh, yeah. But we aren't close."

He seemed to accept the story. "No siblings?"

"No."

"I'm surprised you aren't a brat if you're an only child."

"Wait until you get to know me better."

He laughed. "You have no flaws, Syd."

"I beg to differ."

He finished his food then pushed the plate away. There were still mounds of food on the table. "You're going to eat all of that."

"Maybe in a month," she said.

"I'm being serious. You need to eat if you want to stay strong."

"Just shut up already. I don't eat when I'm depressed."

"So do you overeat when you're happy?"

"I guess."

"Then I'll have to keep you happy."

"Consider it done," she said as she wiped her face with a napkin and pushed it away.

He started to wrap up the food and put in the refrigerator. He was wearing an old shirt and running shorts. She wished he would walk around naked but then they would never leave the bedroom. "What do you want to do today?"

"Stay home with you."

"Sounds good to me."

She placed her dishes in the sink then walked into the bedroom. He followed her a moment later. She grabbed her phone to see if Henry had called. She wanted to know if he was okay with everything.

Coen read her mind. "Give him space."

"I just worry," she said with a sigh.

"Don't." He walked over to the nightstand and sorted through all the condoms. There were at least thirty.

"Do you think we really need all of those?"

He picked up a red packet. "That depends on how quick you can get on the pill."

"I'll go to the clinic on Monday."

"Good. You have no idea how good it feels to not wear anything."

"Well, why don't we just keep pulling out?"

He shook his head. "I did it one time because I wanted it to be special, intimate. I can't risk the chance of knocking you up. We both aren't ready for that."

"I'll be the first one in line when they open."

"Thank you," he said as he pulled his clothes off.

She marveled at the sight of chiseled physique. He looked like he was sculpted by a renowned artist. His statue could be erected in front of museums. His stern jaw and dark stubble made her squeeze her thighs together. She liked it when he didn't shave for a few days.

"Syd?"

"Sorry. What?"

He smiled. "Zoned out there?"

She rubbed her hands on his chest and stomach. "You're just so hot. I kinda forget about everything else." She kissed the skin over his heart. "And I can't believe how much I love you."

"Can I stare at you like that?"

"Sure. It isn't as wonderful a sight as this though."

"When you eat again, it will be." He pulled off the shirt she was wearing then removed her thong. "I don't like lying in bed with clothes on."

"Neither do I."

He laid her on the bed then crawled next to her. "So we are going to do this all weekend?"

"Yep," she said as she cuddled next to him.

"We need to get a TV in here."

"I have all the entertainment I need."

He turned on his side and rested his head close to hers. The look in his eyes told Sydney everything she needed to know. That he loved her more than anything. He didn't need to say it. It was obvious. When she earned a scholarship to come to Hawaii, she was ecstatic to get away from her stepfather, but that joy was nothing compared to this. She loved Coen in a unique way. If he asked her to marry him, she would have a hard time saying no.

"So, we're good, right?" he asked.

"What do you mean?"

"I'm the person you trust most in your life."

"Of course."

"Can I ask you something?"

She felt her heart accelerate, making her muscles spasm with tension. She knew what he would ask and she didn't want to discuss it. It had nothing to do with trust. It was just too painful to speak of. All it would do is bring him pain. She couldn't do that to him.

"Listen to me before you immediately reject me."

She was surprised he read her mind so quickly.

"I'm your boyfriend—your man. It's important to me that I know you are always safe and taken care of. I'm perfectly aware of your strength. I'm not afraid for you to go anywhere by yourself or do anything you want to do. That's not the issue. What bothers me is something clearly frightens you. You've worked with a trainer for two years and you still want to learn more. Whatever made you seek self-defense is obviously serious." She said nothing and looked away. "The fact that you are scared becomes an issue for me. It's my job to protect you, emotionally and physically. Please tell me what has you so scared. Please."

"You told me you wouldn't ask again."

He sighed. "So you still won't tell me?"

"No."

He pressed his forehead against hers, trying to bottle his obvious frustration. "Why not?"

"It will only cause you pain."

"True. But I need to know anyway."

"This isn't fair. You never would have known anything if you weren't my trainer. I don't want to talk about it and I don't want anyone to know. Please drop it."

"What about us?"

"I don't see the relevance."

"I'm the man you love. I want to know everything about you. The good and the bad."

She sighed. She understood his concern came from his love for her. She shouldn't be mad at him. It was something she would want to know as well. "I'm not in danger anymore so there's no need to be concerned. That's all that matters."

"Don't fucking lie to me," he snapped. "I won't tolerate that shit."

She flinched at the venom in his voice.

"You wouldn't continue training if you didn't need it anymore. Don't disrespect me like that ever again."

"I'm sorry."

He said nothing. "I hate to be an asshole, but I'm going to be one for the moment. You will tell me exactly who is scaring you, who gives you nightmares, who makes you seek specialized training so you can actually sleep at night. It will happen."

"I can take care of myself."

"That's beside the point."

"Please let it go."

"I can't."

"I'll tell you when I'm ready to."

He sat up and looked at her. "You promise?"

"Yes."

"When? When we're eighty?"

"Soon. Just please drop it."

"Thank you." He lay back down.

"Can I ask you something?"

"Anything."

"Why did you and Audrey break up?"

"She cheated on me."

"Really?"

"You sound surprised."

"I just assumed—"

"I would be the cheater? No. I did everything for that girl. She got drunk and went to a party then fucked some guy."

"When was this?"

"Seven months ago."

Her heart stopped beating. "With who?"

"I never asked. I didn't want to know."

"Aaron cheated on me seven months ago. He said he was so drunk he couldn't even remember it."

"She had the same story."

"Do you think?"

"That would be ironic."

"It disgusts me that Aaron would sleep with her."

"I couldn't care less."

"Why?"

"She wasn't right for me. If we hadn't broken up, I wouldn't have found you."

She smiled. "That's true."

"Maybe they'll end up together. They are definitely suitable for one another."

"Yuck," Sydney said. "I would hate to end up with her."

7

"She's a stupid bitch."

"Should I be worried about her?"

"What do you mean?" Coen asked.

"Do you think she'll bother me?"

"Don't worry about her. I won't let her bother you."

"Has she talked to you lately?"

He was quiet for a moment. "I thought you didn't want to know about that stuff."

"Well, we were broken up so—"

"I didn't touch her," he said quickly.

She breathed a sigh of relief.

"She came to my parents' house and tried to have dinner with us. When she wouldn't leave, I left."

"You introduced her to your parents?"

"Not really. We ran into my family and that's how they met. I wasn't planning on introducing her for a long time."

"How long were you together?"

"Almost a year."

"Wow."

"What about you and Aaron?"

"About the same."

"I've been happier with you than I ever was with her, even though I've been a fucking secret most of the time."

"I said I was sorry."

"I know, baby. I won't bring it up anymore."

She closed her eyes and let her hand drift down his chest, feeling the rise of his pecs.

"You look beautiful when you sleep," he said suddenly.

"I do?"

"I was going to say it when you woke up this morning, but the first thing you did was starting riding me."

"Are you complaining?"

"Definitely not. I like pleasing you."

"I want to be pleased right now."

"You do?"

She bit her lip as she nodded.

"Your wish is my command."

She pulled him on top of her and wrapped her legs around his waist.

He pinned her hands against the mattress and started kissing her neck then her chin. "How do you want it?"

"However you want to give it."

"You want me to make love to you, slow and steady, or do you want me to fuck you, thrusting into you hard?"

"I want to fuck."

"Will do." He returned to kissing her neck, sucking the skin until he almost bruised it. His lips trailed to her shoulder, kissing the sensitive area. He wanted to ignite her desire in every way possible. When it came to sex, it was about involving everything from her fingers to her toes.

She tried to move her hands but he kept them pinned to the mattress, not letting her touch him. His lips trailed down to her nipples and he kissed each one then sucked hard, making her gasp from both pain and pleasure. When he moved lower down, he kissed her flat stomach. He loved feeling the muscles of her torso. She was strong and hard, not frail like most other girls he'd been with. As he moved further down, her hands started to squeeze his, anticipating his kiss.

She opened her legs wider, welcoming his tongue inside of her. She took a deep breath and moaned as his tongue darted into her folds. She was writhing on the bed, unable to stay still even if she wanted to. His tongue made her feel things she never felt before. It moved around her clitoris then returned to her wet pussy. He continued to please her. His hot breath blew inside her and she moaned again at the feel of him. Her insides burned with desire so much that she felt panicked. She wanted him and she wanted him now.

"Please," she begged, still trapped under his hands.

He continued to kiss her down below, making her legs shake. Her taste was sweet, making him hard. Knowing how much she enjoyed it got him excited, more aroused than he already was. He brought her to the very edge, the threshold of her orgasm, and when she started to shake, moaning incoherently, he pulled away.

She grabbed a condom quicker than he could move and ripped it open. He climbed on top of her immediately, letting her roll the condom onto his cock. It was a tight fit. She was practically drooling as she stared at it, wanting to get fucked more than he wanted to fuck her. She pulled the tip and made sure he had plenty of room. Because of all the jizz that came out the night before, she gave him a little extra space.

As soon as she released him, he grabbed her hips and pinned her legs back, sliding into her quickly. She gasped loudly, pleased by the sudden stretching of her insides. He didn't start gentle like last time. He fucked her hard and fast, slamming her headboard against the wall.

He moved further over her until her legs were practically behind her head, thrusting into her with long, even strokes. She grabbed his ass, asking him to go faster than he already was.

She laid her head back on the pillow and watched him fuck her vigorously. She took it thrust by thrust and bit her lip to keep from screaming. She was in heaven, loving the feeling of him move into her in just the right away. The bed creaked like it would break but she really didn't care. The sensation started in the pit of her stomach and moved to the area between her legs. It was hot and fiery, hotter than the inside of a spewing volcano. She felt her body tighten as the orgasm spread through her body. She tightened around him, increasing the friction as he moved. She knew he felt it when he grunted, "Fuck." She screamed as she grabbed his ass, moving with him harder as she enjoyed every passing second of her orgasm. It was so good it made her head spin. She closed her eyes for a moment as her body took a break and recharged.

"Make me come again," she said through her heavy breathing.

He slowed down as he grabbed her legs and placed them over his shoulders. He leaned back on the balls of his feet and moved into her, hitting her as deep as her body would allow. The position felt fuller and made her eyes roll to the back of her head. She usually lost all arousal after she came once, but he always kept her horny. She didn't want this to end. She could do this all day.

Coen was grateful he wore a condom because it was hard not to come so early when it was skin to skin. Sex was more satisfying with her because he loved her so much. She brought his orgasm to the surface as soon as they touched. Most of the time, he was trying not to come so he could please her. She was the perfect size and perfect length for him to slide in and out. She was tight but not too tight. If she were a virgin, this would have taken a few times until she could actually enjoy it. But there was no doubt that she enjoyed him from the start. The movement of her tits was enough to set him off. He held it back even though his pleasure started building in his balls. He wanted her to come so he moved into her harder, giving her everything he had. Thankfully, she started to moan his name over and over. That was his cue. He closed his eyes and thrust into her, feeling himself come in the tip of the condom. He couldn't wait to actually come inside her without any friction. When he and Audrey stopped using condoms, it took him a long time to get used to it enough to last long. She was frustrated with him for a while but he did the best he could. When Sydney started taking the pill, he would have to masturbate regularly if he was going to make her come even once. Last night was a miracle. He was too determined to make it perfect for her to let himself come too soon.

Sydney grabbed him and pulled him to her. "I love you so much, Coen."

"I love you too."

"Don't pull out yet."

"Why?"

"I like feeling you."

He kissed her forehead. "I'm going to be inside more often than I'm outside of you if we keep this up."

"Good."

He rubbed his nose against hers. "I love being loved."

"You're the most amazing man I've ever met, besides my father."

"Thank you."

"But I do love fucking you. I can't lie about it. I fantasized about you before I even spoke to you. I thought about you in so many sexual ways."

"That's perfectly okay," he said as he smiled at her. "I want you to feel that way. But I like knowing there is more to this relationship than that."

"A lot more."

"You can have me whenever you want me. I hope the feeling is mutual."

"Yes, definitely."

"Because I fantasized about you after I met you. I had a lot of wet dreams."

"That's so hot."

"You don't think I'm a pervert?"

"I want you to be a pervert."

"Well, I enjoy fucking you and I think about it every day. I can't count the number of times I thought about your naked body when I jacked off in the middle of the night or in the shower. I have tissues for days."

She groaned. "Now I want to have sex again."

"Give me a few minutes," he said with a laugh.

She held him to her chest and closed her eyes. "I'm so glad this happened."

"Me too."

She sighed happily.

"Would you like to do something?"

"Fuck."

"Besides that."

"You wanna go out to dinner?"

"I would love to take you out."

"Okay."

"What do we do until then?"

"Lie here."

"Sounds good." He pulled out of her and she whimpered as if she was in pain. He pulled the condom off then threw it in the wastebasket. "This room is going to smell like sex soon."

"I like that scent."

He lay beside her and wrapped her in his arms. "So why do you want to be a marine biologist?"

She shrugged. "I love animals."

"Is that why you're a vegetarian?"

She made a face. "Please don't give me shit for it."

"Not at all. As long as you still have a balanced diet, I don't care what you eat." He tapped her thigh. "You obviously get enough protein."

"Will you be my trainer again?"

"Of course. But let's do it in private so you don't have to pay me."

"I don't mind paying you."

"I don't want your money," he said quickly.

"Okay."

He held her to his chest then closed his eyes. "Sorry. I get really tired after I come."

"I do too."

She ran her fingers through his hair and stared at his face. His mouth relaxed and formed a thin line. The stubble around his chin was rough to the touch. When she brushed it with her fingertips, it felt coarse under her fingertips. She explored him, feeling each strand of hair and every inch of his skin, mesmerized by the perfection of his face. He was the most handsome man she had ever seen. She was always attracted to him in a physical way, but now she felt completely infatuated with him. He was everything to her. Perhaps she should just tell him the truth about her horrific past. She was afraid he would judge her, maybe not even want to be with her anymore. But in her heart, she knew he loved her. She believed him.

2

When they woke up, it was dark outside. Sydney never spent her day lying around, sleeping, but she enjoyed doing nothing with him. The time went by so fast. Whenever she was bored and alone, time seemed to move so slowly. With him, everything was different.

He opened his eyes then looked at her, seeing that she was exactly where he left her. "Hello, beautiful."

She ran her hands across his chest and gave him that look she always gave him when she wanted him. He recognized it immediately. The movement of her hand across his chest and the way she stared at his body told him everything he needed to know. She moved on top of him, kissing his chest and stomach. Every touch of her lips made him more aroused. He already had morning wood even though it was nighttime. She didn't need to do anything else to keep him excited. Just seeing her naked was enough to make him pop a boner.

He grabbed her face and pulled her to him. "How do you want it?"

"You pick this time."

"I can only make you come once."

"That's fine," she said as she ran her hands up his chest.

"Turn over." She did as he commanded and stuck her ass out to him.

The tight curve of her ass and her perfect thighs made his cock twitch. Her body was perfect in every way. He hated girls that were skinny and weak. She was toned and muscular, having the strength to throw a punch that could break someone's nose. Her strength was a turn on for him. The view was so beautiful that he wanted to enjoy it for a moment. When he pressed his fingers to her pussy, he felt how wet she was. She was ready for him and very eager. It amazed him how she wanted him all the time. Girls wanted him to fuck their brains out, but never like this. This was a first.

He laid his chest on her back, feeling her smooth skin pressed against him. She was warm and inviting. He pulled her hair to one side of her shoulder and kissed her exposed neck, rubbing his dick in between her ass cheeks. She moaned quietly as he kissed her, slightly moving with him. He kissed her ear. "Beautiful." His hands ran down her back and massaged her muscles, making her more relaxed. He liked foreplay because it made her come quick. Fucking her from behind, it was hard not to come so fast. With an ass like that, it was almost impossible.

He leaned down and kissed her wet pussy gently then inserted his tongue inside her. Her loud moan filled his ear as he pulled away. He leaned back then pressed his mouth against her ear. "You taste sweet." He wrapped his arm around her and squeezed her breasts, pinching the nipples slightly. Her panting increased and he felt the moisture from her wet pussy as he pressed against her. He knew she wanted him bad. "I'm almost done. Be patient."

"Coen," she said with a moan.

He leaned back and grabbed her hips, staring at her ass. He really wanted to fuck her without a condom but he knew he shouldn't.

"It's okay," she said, reading his mind. "Do it."

"I won't last long."

17

"You can do it."

His sex crazed mind got the better of him. He really wanted to fuck her and feel every single groove over her insides. He wanted to feel the delicate texture of her skin, the hot moisture of her pussy. He pressed the tip of cock, which was already leaking, and slipped it inside. He shook as he slid inside her completely with one stroke. The initial contact was enough to make him come if he wanted to. He leaned over her, pressing his chest against her back, and pressed his tongue to her ear while he slowly moved inside her. "Don't move," he said with a shaky breath. "Don't make any noises. Tell me when you are done coming."

"Oh—okay."

He leaned back on his heels and stared at her ass while he thrust inside of her, pushing his tip as far as it would go before he pulled it out. His orgasm was in the base of his balls, ready to spring at a moment's notice. They were silent. Only the sound of the springing coils of the bed could be heard as he moved into her gently. He could feel everything inside of her. It felt too fucking good. He was gasping in seconds, shaking with unbelievable pleasure. When he felt her tighten around him, he gasped again, knowing she was coming. She stayed quiet like he asked. When she started moaning and screaming his name, it was hard not to release.

"I'm done."

He fucked her hard and fast, letting himself explode. When his come was about to shoot out, he pulled out and humped her ass cheeks, letting it spray all over her back. Moving from the welcoming warmth of her pussy to the cold sting of the air was a quick shock, but he still came hard. He was left wheezing and gasping for breath, unable to control his lungs or his body. He went from never having sex to fucking every hour, and his body wasn't used to it.

He grabbed a towel and wiped the jizz from her back. It was everywhere but he cleaned it up and in a few strokes.

When she lay down, she reached for him. "I want you to come inside me."

"You have no idea how much I want to."

"I can't wait."

He rubbed his nose against hers. "Me too."

"You still want to go out to dinner?"

"We have to get out of this house."

"Let's take a shower."

He eyed her suspiciously. "I'm not a machine."

"I'll be good, I promise."

"At this rate, we won't need condoms. I'll just shoot blanks."

Her eyes shined. "That sounds good. Let's do that."

They got into the shower together, letting the hot water run across their bodies. Coen grabbed a bottle of body wash and squeezed it into his hands. He rubbed it across Sydney's body, massaging it into her skin and shoulders. When he rubbed the soap across her breasts, his dick twitched. "You've got to be kidding me."

She turned around and saw his erection. "What a lovely surprise."

"How is this possible? We already did it twice."

She grabbed him and stroked him with shampoo, making him twitch harder. "Well, he wants to do it again."

Her ministrations were making him breathless. "I hope you don't mind having a late dinner."

"Fuck dinner," she said as she rubbed him harder.

He swallowed the lump in his throat as she jerked him. She ran her fingers through his hair while she kissed him, feeling his lips with her own. His lips stopped moving and he just breathed into her mouth, letting her rub her thumb over his tip as she moved up. When she touched his balls gently, he felt his hands shake. He wrapped his arms around her, leaving them on her ass. He squeezed it as she tightened her fingers around his shaft.

"Stop. I'm gonna come."

"I want you to."

"No. I want to get you off."

"You can after dinner."

"But—"

"Shut up and come for me."

He surrendered and pressed his forehead against hers, staring at her breasts while he rubbed her ass. Her tits giggled as she stroked him harder, making the nipples harden. It was nice not to worry about pulling out or getting her off. It was a relief, actually. He tried to control himself so the hand job would last longer, but it was useless. When the orgasm started, he didn't fight it. It came out and splashed on her skin, but she kept rubbing him until he was completely done.

He gasped for breath, holding her close to him.

She rubbed his back and trailed her fingers along his sides, helping him relax from his post sex high. Her nails glided through his hair, feeling the wet strands. Steam rose around them, making them feel warm and uncomfortable. "You don't always have to get me off."

"I like getting you off," he said as he pulled away.

"I want you to feel as much pleasure as I do."

"Well, I did like that."

"How about a blow job?"

He moaned. "I would love one."

"Maybe after dinner," she said as she kissed him.

"I look forward to it."

They finished their shower then dried off and got ready for their date. Sydney wore a light sundress that was dark blue with red Hawaiian flowers. She wore a gold bracelet that contrasted against the dark color of her skin tone. In California, she was always pale in the winter, but here she was dark all year round.

When she walked into the living room, Coen was wearing long shorts and a black shirt, which showed the muscles of his chest and arms. He looked at her.

"Wow," he said as he rose from the couch. "You look exceptional."

"Thank you."

He kissed her neck then her shoulders, running his hands up her dress. "I like this on you."

"You do?"

"Yeah." He grabbed her ass underneath her dress, fingering her thong. "I like it when you wear dresses."

"I don't usually wear them."

"You should. You look gorgeous."

She blushed. "Thank you."

"I don't know if we're going to make it to the restaurant now, not after you pulled a stunt like this."

"A stunt like what?"

"Wearing this," he said as he felt the material. "Who are you trying to fool?"

"I just wanted to look nice."

"The objective has been met."

"Let's go before you rip this off."

"I'll rip it off when we get home."

They left the house then climbed into his Tacoma. He placed his arm over the backseat as he backed out of the driveway and headed to the restaurants on the coast. She placed her hand on his thigh, dangerously close to his crotch and leaned against him. He turned on the radio and they listened to indie rock on the drive. They said nothing for the journey, but the silence wasn't awkward or uncomfortable. Neither one had anything to say.

They arrived at the restaurant and Coen walked her to the front, holding her hand. "For two, please."

"Of course, sir," the waitress said as she led them to a table by the window.

Coen pulled out Sydney's chair for her then moved to his seat across the table. When Sydney picked up the menu, she was pleased to see a wide selection of vegetarian items. There were too many to choose from, actually.

"Baby, what are you getting?"

She blushed. She loved it when he called her that. He didn't say it all the time, just once in a while, but she still enjoyed it when he decided to use the affectionate nickname. "I can't decide."

"I think I'm going to get the fish."

She nodded, unsure what to say. Nothing with meat sounded appetizing to her. "I'm going to get pasta. That's always good."

"Excellent choice."

The waitress came to their table and Coen ordered for the both of them. "Also, can we have two glasses of your house wine?"

"Yes, sir."

"Thank you," he said before she walked away. He turned to Sydney. "I hope you don't mind about the wine. I want you to try it. I think you'll like it."

"Or you are trying to get me drunk."

He laughed. "I can barely keep your legs closed as it is."

"That's not my fault."

"Well, it isn't mine."

"Yes, it is. You are so sexy and perfect."

"Perfect? I was failing zoology. Remember?"

"But you were distracted."

"But I still failed it. I'm definitely not perfect."

"Why couldn't you concentrate that day? I've always wanted to ask you that."

The waitress brought their water and their wine. He waited until she walked away before he responded.

"I had an argument with Audrey."

"About what?"

He swirled the wine before he sipped it. "After she cheated on me, I took her back like an idiot. That day, she begged me to give her a third chance and she wouldn't stop pestering me. She slapped me so hard, I had a headache all day. I was just depressed and upset. It all happened right before the exam."

"I think hitting your partner is unacceptable, regardless of their sex."

"I agree—except when we're training."

She felt the anger course through her body. "That isn't right, babe."

He smiled, moved by the possessive name. "It's okay. She's done it so many times that I'm used to it."

"That just pisses me off even more."

"I'm fine. It didn't hurt."

"I really want to slap that bitch."

"I won't stop you."

She crossed her arms over her chest and breathed through her anger. The idea of someone hitting Coen, who was the sweetest guy she ever met, sent her to the brink. Even if a woman was responsible for the hit, it still made her angry. He didn't deserve to be treated like that.

He noticed the tension in her shoulders. "Don't let it bother you. Try some wine." He pushed her glass closer to her.

She picked it up and sipped it. It was good, not too sweet and not too tart. "It's good."

"Have you ever been drunk before?"

"No."

"Because you don't like alcohol or because you know your limits?"

"I hardly drink alcohol because I don't trust myself. My mom was a mean drunk and I probably am too." She let that fact slip from her lips without thinking. That was something she never told anyone. He didn't react at all, bringing the glass to his lips for another drink. "And I just couldn't trust anyone to not take advantage of me except Henry, and he wasn't always there. It just gives me peace of mind when I don't drink at all."

"You're drinking now."

"I know you'll take care of me. And it's just a glass of wine—nothing too crazy."

"Would you like to get drunk? See if you are a crazy drunk?"

"Not really."

"What if we stayed home and it was just us two?"

She shrugged. "Maybe."

"I won't let you do anything stupid and if you are mean to me, I'll put up with it."

"Why would you want to do that?"

"Because I know you aren't a mean drunk. I just want to prove it to you."

"How do you know that?"

"Most people aren't that different when they're drunk. Yes, their emotions are heightened and they have less inhibition, but they really aren't different people. You are friendly, quiet, and mellow. You would probably be the same if you were drunk. You definitely wouldn't start cursing at everyone and throwing swings."

"What are you like when you're drunk?"

"People tell me I laugh a lot."

"So you are fun?"

"I guess."

"That's a bad combination. A fun drunk and a mean one."

"You wouldn't be a mean drunk."

25

"We'll see."

The waitress brought their food. "Do you need anything else?"

"Can we have a bottle of this wine to go?"

"Of course." She walked away.

Sydney raised an eyebrow. "You want to do this tonight?"

"Not necessarily. It'll be there if you ever decide to."

"I drink Tequila sometimes. It helps me sleep."

"How much were you drinking?"

"Half a bottle straight."

"Wait. What? When was this?"

She was quiet for a moment. "When you were gone."

He sighed. "Don't ever do that again, Sydney."

"Okay," she said automatically. She cut into her pasta and took a bite. Coen ate his dinner with grace, never spilling anything on the table or hardly using his napkin. When she was finished, she wiped her mouth with the napkin then placed it on the table. She stared at Coen across from her, admiring the beauty of his features.

"What are you thinking about?"

"What I always think about."

He smiled. "Damn. I am good."

"That's an understatement."

"I wonder if I'll ever tame you."

"I find it unlikely."

"That's just as well."

The waitress brought the tab and Coen slid the money into the sleeve, handing it back to her. "I don't need any change."

Sydney watched her walk away. "Since we are in a relationship, I would like to take turns paying for things."

"No."

"No?"

"That's never going to happen."

"Why?"

"You're my lady. I take care of you."

"We are both in college, totally broke."

"I'm not broke. My parents pay for my education and I make plenty of money as a trainer. I could get my own place without roommates, I just choose to live with other people so I can save more money. I pay for everything. That's settled."

She glared at him. "I don't accept that."

"Too bad," he said as he rose to a stand. He grabbed the bottle of wine then her hand. They left the restaurant and returned to the car, placing the bottle in the back seat. "Let's walk on the beach."

She crossed her arms over her chest as she walked beside him.

He wrapped his arm around her waist. "Come on, Syd. Don't be mad."

"I'm a feminist. I believe in an equal partnership. I want to carry my own weight."

"You do. You make love to me. That's worth more than cash."

"You make love to me too. We're even in that department. This is a give and take relationship. Get used to it. I won't change my mind."

He sighed. "Look, I understand what you're saying and I respect it. When we get married, we can split bills and all that junk, but when we go out, I would like to treat you."

"When we get married?"

"I don't mean right now, but someday."

"You want to get married someday?"

He raised an eyebrow. "I told you I loved you, didn't I? I only date women that I'm serious about, women that I can actually see myself marrying. If I didn't feel that way, I would just sleep with you then take off."

"So you wanted to marry Audrey?"

"In the beginning of the relationship, I could see it. But after that, definitely not. I was trying to end the relationship more than I was trying to keep it together. When she cheated on me, I knew she didn't love me. She just liked fucking me." He looked at her. "But I do want to marry you. There's no doubt about that. I know I'm not going to change my mind."

She said nothing for a long time. "I feel the same way."

He smiled. "Good. I know I said that I loved Audrey at one point, but when I think about my feelings for you, I realize I never did. And if I did, it pales in comparison to my love for you."

"I feel the same way about Aaron."

He grabbed her hand and they continued to walk on the beach, kicking up sand with their toes. "So, is that okay?"

"What?"

"That I pay for everything?"

"I still don't like it. I don't pay rent and my tuition is free. All the money I make at the aquarium goes into my savings account. I have money too."

He sighed. "I'll feel more comfortable if I take care of you. I want to take care of you. Please let me do that."

"But I don't need someone to take care of me."

"Then humor me."

"Fine."

He smiled. "Thank you."

They looked at the water as it shined under the moon. Her dress flapped in the wind, showing her legs under the dress.

"You really don't need someone to take care of you?" he asked sadly. "Because I need you to take care of me."

She looked at him. "I meant in terms of financial stability. Coen, I do need you to take care of me in other ways, in ways that money can never buy. I've never called anyone, sobbing, and asked them to come to me. I've never been that weak before."

"It's not weak, Syd."

"It feels like it."

"As soon as I find myself on hard times, you'll be the first person I run to. You are a safe haven to me."

She smiled. "You're my safe haven too."

"When Brutus died, I cried for days. I'm not ashamed to admit it. If people think it makes me look weak, I really don't care. I loved someone with my whole heart and then I lost him. When you called me, it was brave to open yourself up like that, exposing yourself to vulnerability. I knew he would die one day. I still loved him anyway."

She watched him as he walked next to her, his eyes on a distant memory.

"And when the dreams that haunt you come and frighten you, it's okay to be scared. It's okay to reach for me. I'm not going to judge you for it. I just wish you would tell me what frightens you so much. I know you don't believe me, but I can help you get through it and move on. I suspect you won't tell me because you chose to push it to the back of your mind, hoping it would go away on its own. I can tell you right now that it won't." She averted her gaze. "I've had clients that were beaten and assaulted in the streets. When they finally came to me, they told me what happened. They were afraid to tell their loved ones to spare them the pain, but when they were talking to me, it was therapeutic." She still didn't say anything. "I'm not pressuring you to tell me what haunts you. I'm just saying that you'll feel better once you do."

"You're probably right."

"I am right."

3

When they got home, they went straight into the bedroom, leaving the bottle of wine on the couch, forgotten.

Coen touched the straps of her dress and slipped each one off until the dress fell to the floor. He pressed his forehead against hers as he unclasped her bra and let it fall. When she was just standing in her underwear, he kissed her body everywhere, relishing the taste of her skin. "Give me a minute," he whispered into her ear. He licked his tongue across her neck then down her shoulder, making her spine shiver. Then, he grabbed her breasts and squeezed them gently, cupping them in his large hands. His eyes were wide with excitement as he explored her. It didn't matter how many times he had done it. He was still obsessed with touching her everywhere. The tan color of her skin reminded him of a golden pineapple. Sunkissed. Her skin was soft and smooth even though she swam in the ocean almost every day. Her hands weren't calloused even though she worked as a custodian. She was a direct contradiction to everything she did. When his hands glided down her ribs, he saw a thin line, almost impossible to see. It looked like a scratch. He caressed it with his fingers while she looked at him, waiting for him to comment on it. When he didn't, she tried not to look relieved.

Tired of waiting for him to finish, she stripped off his clothes and studied his body. His skin was flawless even though he was a trainer and had been in more physical sparring matches than she would ever know. He flexed his chest muscles when she touched him, showing her he was strong. He didn't need to do that because she already knew how muscular he was. He just liked to prove a point. There was no trace of damage anywhere on his body. He was lucky he escaped unscathed. "You're so beautiful," she said as she felt his broad shoulders. "And not just on the outside."

"There's no comparison," he said as he kissed her gently, parting her lips with his tongue. His tongue danced around hers. The parting of their lips and the quiet moans fell on their ears, exciting both of them. He guided her to the bed then laid her down, crawling on top of her. She opened her legs and felt him push against her.

She broke their kiss. "Lie down."

He read her mind. He knew she wanted to go down on him. "I want to make love."

"You do?"

"I'm so in love with you," he said as he kissed her.

Hot tears sprang from her eyes and one dripped down her cheek. The emotion escaped for a moment then disappeared in light of their passion. She could never find the words to explain how she felt about him, how she loved him.

Her hands ran down his back, memorizing every muscle under his skin. She knew his body better than he did. When he breathed into her mouth, she felt even more excited. The heat was always there between them. Just a kiss was enough to light a fire in between her legs. He always sent her to the edge of pleasure, almost making her come before they actually had sex. Before he actually entered inside her, she was brewing with sexual frustration. She grabbed a condom then ripped it open. He leaned over her and let her roll it onto his cock. It twitched as she touched it. When she squeezed him gently then ran her thumb over the tip, he moaned quietly. He inserted the tip inside her, pushing his large head entirely in, before he made the plunge. As soon as he was fully inside her, she felt her walls crumble.

"I'm coming already."

He moved into her harder, kissing her while he ran his hands through her hair.

She scratched his back, digging her nails into his skin as her body shook with her high. It felt so good every time. She bit her lip as she moaned loudly, feeling him move inside until her orgasm was completely gone.

Coen locked his eyes onto hers, moving into her slowly and deeply. Just because she came didn't mean he wanted this to end. He never wanted their lovemaking to end. She was the most amazing girl he'd ever met in his life. She was the one, his everything. He'd never had a friend who meant as much to him, a girlfriend he loved more than his own family, or a lover that satisfied all of his needs. For him, there was nobody else. She was it.

Tears sprang from his eyes as the emotion rocked through him. "I love you so much, Sydney."

She touched his face, kissing his tears away. "I love you, Coen."

When his body started to shake, he knew he couldn't hold on much longer. The moment was too perfect and pure for him to contain it anymore. He stared into her eyes as he came inside her, completely depleting himself. The orgasm felt good, but the feeling in his heart felt better. He had never been broken, but now he felt completely whole. He didn't realize something was missing in his heart until now. She was the missing piece to his tower. The small but irreplaceable part that completed the entire piece, arranged the entire puzzle. She was the muse to his painting, the light to the stars, the moon to the sky.

He pulled out then lay beside her, his heart still heavy with emotion. He pulled off the condom then tossed it in the trash before he held her to his chest, squeezing her so tightly he thought he would explode. Sydney saw the depth of his love for her. It was obvious.

She knew she had to tell him the truth of her past. It would hurt them both but they could get through it together. He would still love her and want her just as much as he did now. In fact, he may love her more.

4

When they woke up the next morning, they were tangled in each other's arms. Sydney opened her eyes first and looked at Coen. He was breathing deeply and peacefully. Even though she had to pee, she didn't want to wake him up so she didn't move.

A few minutes later, his eyes opened. He turned his head and looked at her, delighted to see her face right when he woke up. He placed his hand on her cheek and stoked it with his thumb.

"Hi," she said.

He cleared his throat. "Morning."

"You sleep well?"

"Really well. How about you?"

"I've never slept better in my life than when I started sleeping with you."

"I'm glad I could help."

"I don't have nightmares with you."

"Because I'm your dream catcher."

She grabbed his hand and kissed it. "And so much more."

"I'm going to shower and get ready," he said as he rubbed the sleep from his eyes.

"I'll reheat breakfast. We need to eat it all."

"*You* need to eat it all."

"I ate all my dinner last night."

"That isn't enough."

"Do you want me to be fat?"

"I want you to be healthy."

"I'm fine, babe."

He kissed her on the head before walking in the bathroom. She stared at his ass as he walked away. She heard the toilet flush and then the shower run. She decided to tell him the truth after breakfast. It was time.

When he was finished getting ready, he joined her at the kitchen table for breakfast. He ate two helpings before he was done then drank two cups of coffee—black. "What do you want to do today, baby?"

"Can we sit on the beach?"

"Whatever my lady wants to do is fine with me."

She carried the plates to the sink and rinsed them before she loaded the dishwasher. She changed into shorts and a shirt then fixed her hair before they walked down to the water, hand in hand. They got their feet wet as the waves covered their ankles. After they played around and looked for crabs and seahorses, they walked to the sand and sat down.

Coen leaned close to her, his shoulder touching hers. He picked up a stick and doodled in the sand. Sydney watched him for a moment until she realized what he drew. *I love Sydney.* He erased it then redrew it.

She squeezed her hands together as she organized her thoughts. It was harder than she thought it was going to be. She never told anyone that horror story before. Henry was her best friend but he had no idea that she experienced anything so traumatizing. She was determined to take it to the grave—until Coen.

"Coen, I'm ready to talk."

He dropped the stick, forgetting the drawing. "I'm ready to listen." He looked out at the ocean, not smothering her with too much attention. Sometimes that scared people off.

Sydney looked at the sand below her feet. "Before I tell you, you have to promise me a few things."

"I'll do whatever you wish."

"I'm being serious."

"I know, baby. What do you want me to promise?"

"You can't kill anyone."

His eyes widened in shock. "Now I'm worried."

"Coen," she pressed.

He sighed. "I promise."

"You can't hurt anyone."

"That depends on the context of the situation. If someone is trying to hurt you, I will intervene and beat them senseless. I refuse to make the promise."

"You can defend me or defend yourself. You can't seek anyone out with cruel intentions."

"Okay. I promise."

"You can't judge me."

"That's a given. I would never do that."

"You can't run away from me."

"I would never do that either."

"Promise me you'll still love me."

He grabbed her hand and put it over his heart. "With my whole heart."

"This last one you'll have the most difficulty with."

"Thanks for the warning."

"You can't get mad."

He was quiet for a moment. "I can't get mad?"

"You have to stay calm and be understanding. If you flip out, then I'm going to fall apart."

"I need a minute."

"Okay."

He stared out at the ocean for a long time, pondering her request. It was difficult to make such a promise without the information beforehand. He knew it was bad and it would break his heart. But Sydney was right. He had to be strong and collected for her, to help her put the past behind her. "I promise," he said quietly.

She took a deep breath. "Okay."

"It's going to be okay, Sydney. You'll feel better afterwards."

"Not right afterwards."

"Come on, baby." He held her hand in his own and caressed her knuckles.

"Well, when my dad died, my mom remarried right away. I suspect she was cheating on Dad because it happened so quickly."

"How soon?"

"Two months."

"I would make the same guess."

"My stepdad isn't a good person. He's a drunken bastard that lacks any intelligence whatsoever. He can't even argue logically because that ability is completely gone. Anything could set him off. The opening of the refrigerator door, a press conference with the president on the television, the color shirt I'm wearing—anything. I was too afraid to leave my room most of the time when he sat in the living room and watched TV. If he saw me, he would start arguing with me, just to argue. It never made sense. If I stood up for myself, the repercussions were always horrific. He would beat me with his hands, and when that wasn't enough, he always used his bat." Coen squeezed her hand but said nothing. "I've been knocked unconscious too many times to remember. He broke two of my ribs, which were fixed. That's what that line is." He nodded. "As I got older, I was able to avoid him better, but for my younger years, I was trapped. I didn't have any birthday parties and never went anywhere with my friends because I wasn't allowed to do anything. It was a dark period for me, years of my life that I'll never get back." Tears started to fall from her eyes. "The worst part was my mom. She never did anything to help me, letting me take the blame for her mistakes most of the time. If she broke something of his, she would let me take the beating for it. I swear to god that bitch never loved me." Coen stared at the ground while he listened to her, hiding any emotion he felt. "I applied to Hawaii University simply because it was an island away from home. I knew they wouldn't be able to afford to visit me and I would be free of them—and his son." She paused for a moment. "Johnny was the worst. When my stepfather wasn't making my life miserable, his son was there to take his place. I think I may hate him more."

"What did he do to you?" he asked with a weak voice, his gaze averted.

"Sexual things. When I told my mom about it, she did nothing, calling me a liar. I woke up in the middle of the night with his finger down my pants. He told me if I said anything, he would tell his dad and he would beat me. So I did nothing, letting him take advantage of me. When I get older, I fought back, disgusted with him. When he told his dad that I was misbehaving, my stepfather would beat me. But it was worth the pain. I would rather be punched and kicked than be fingered by a disgusting pervert. The last thing I did before I left California was break two of his fingers. I know he'll get retribution for that eventually. That's my story."

Coen said nothing, still staring at the sand while he held her hand. He seemed calm and in control, but she knew him better than that. A war was raging inside him, wanting to explode. The retelling of the story did make her feel better. She didn't feel like the grief was only her burden, but his as well.

"Thank you for telling me," he whispered. His eyes were lined with red and a few tears escaped. He blocked his face and looked away before she could get a good look at him. When he felt he had regained control of his emotions, he turned to her and wrapped her in his arms, holding her to his chest. "You're safe now. That's all the matters."

"I know."

"I'll never let either one of them touch you again. I promise you."

"I know, Coen."

"I'm so sorry you had to suffer through that."

"I don't have to suffer alone anymore."

"No, you don't. I can't believe you became such an amazing person through all that grief. It's truly astounding."

"My father. He raised me to control my mind. Nothing else mattered. As long as they couldn't take my mind, thoughts, and beliefs away, I would stay sane. They could have my body."

"Sydney, it wasn't your fault he passed away. It was a horrific accident that was completely out of your control."

"It is my fault."

He looked into her eyes. "If the situation was reversed, would you want your daughter to feel this way? Carrying all this guilt for the rest of her life? Even if it was your fault, it wouldn't change anything. He would want you to be happy, Sydney. It was a tragic accident. It could have happened to anyone."

She nodded. "You're right. I wouldn't want my child to live in regret for the rest of their life."

He kissed her forehead. "So let it go. He would want you to."

She started to sob. "You're right, you're right."

He rocked her back and forth and held her while she sobbed her heart out, remembering all the pain and suffering she experienced through those painful years. She didn't know how long she sat there but hours seemed to trickle by. Coen never removed his arms from around her. He just whispered words of love into her ear.

When she finally felt calm, he pressed his lips to her ear. "I'm your family now, Sydney. I will take care of you as long as you'll have me."

"My family?"

He rubbed his nose against hers. "Yes. Henry, Nancy, and I are your family. Those pieces of shit you used to live with hold no sway over you anymore. You belong with me."

"I've always wanted a real family," she said through her increased breathing.

"And we'll make one of our own."

"We will?"

"Yes."

"You still love me?"

"Always, baby. Always."

"I was so scared that you wouldn't."

"That's impossible."

"Even after what I said about Johnny?"

"It changes nothing, Sydney. Your past is in the past—where it belongs."

"You're right. I do feel better."

"Together, we can get through this and make it a distant memory."

She nodded. "Thank you for not getting mad."

He didn't respond to her comment. "Can I ask you a few things?"

"Yeah."

"What other sexual things did he do to you?" Her eyes widened in fright. "It doesn't change how I feel about you. I just want to know."

"He went down on me."

"He never had sex with you?"

"He tried."

"Do you have any proof?"

"I wish."

"What about your stepdad? Do you have any proof of his crimes?"

"No. I was never allowed to have a cell phone. I would have recorded it if I could."

He sighed. "Then perhaps we should just let it go."

She nodded. "I think that's best."

"We're going to have a beautiful life together, Sydney."

"We haven't been together very long."

"No, we haven't. But I'm never letting you go."

"I don't want you to."

"Good." He rocked her in his arms.

Sydney knew she should tell him about Thanksgiving and how her stepdad and brother planned to fly there, but she didn't want to discuss that yet. She just dropped a bomb on him. He was taking the information so well but she didn't want to push him. One horrific story was enough for the day.

5

When Sydney came to campus the next morning, Henry was just getting out of his car.

"Hey," she said happily as she approached him.

"Hey," he said with a smile. The light was still gone from his eyes. She knew his smile was just a show the second she looked at him. He was still sad. "How was your weekend?"

"It was good," she said awkwardly, thinking about making love all over the place. "How was yours?"

"Great. I went out with some friends and met this girl. We are going out tonight."

"Really? That's great."

"Yeah," he said. "She's cute and—well—Derek made me."

She laughed. "He gave you a little nudge?"

"More like a shove. He walked up to her and said I told him she was the most beautiful woman I had ever seen then introduced her to me. I was forced to go along with it."

"Well, it worked."

"Yeah," he said as he ran his fingers through his hair, shifting his weight. "So, how's Coen?"

She was quiet, unsure what to say.

"Syd, he was going to come up at some point. It's best just to rip off the bandage."

"He's good."

"So, you worked everything out?"

"Yeah. We did."

He nodded. "I'm glad that I was able to repair some of the damage I caused."

"It wasn't your fault, Henry."

"Yes, it was. I feel horrible for pressuring you repeatedly then kissing you when you were heartbroken. I feel like a total ass. If I had known you were with Coen, or even liked the guy, I never would have said anything to you."

"I know, Henry. Please don't apologize. I don't blame you for anything and neither does Coen."

"Really?"

"Of course."

He sighed. "I'm relieved. I was worried about what you thought of me."

"I still think you are a really great guy."

"Okay."

Coen parked his car then jumped out, closing the door behind him.

Henry saw him. "Well, I'll see you later."

"Please don't do that."

"What?"

"You don't have to disappear just because he's around."

Henry put his hands in his pockets and sighed. "I just don't want to come between you guys again."

"You won't. You are always welcome around us."

"Okay."

Coen reached them. "Hey, man," he said as he nodded to Henry. "Have a good weekend?"

"I got a date."

"Ooh. Is she cute?"

"Really cute," he said with a nod.

Coen kissed Sydney on the cheek. "Good morning, baby."

"Hey."

He placed his arm around her. "Let's get to class."

Henry watched them for a moment before he averted his gaze and walked alongside them. It was a little awkward even though she wished it wasn't. It would take some time for Henry to get used to her relationship with Coen.

They took their seats in their classroom but Coen sat next to Sydney with Henry on her other side. When Nancy sat down, she looked at Sydney and smiled. Sydney smiled back.

Sydney leaned toward Coen's ear, whispering so low he could barely hear her. "Please don't be too affectionate with me in front of Henry."

He sighed. "Okay. What does that entail?"

"Just hand holding."

"Okay."

"I'm sorry."

"I understand. As long as he knows we're together, I can do this."

"Thank you," she said with a smile.

"You're lucky I love you so much."

"The luckiest girl in the world."

He smiled at her, conveying all of his love in the look alone. The classroom was an inappropriate place to be affectionate so their stares would have to suffice as intimacy.

Professor Jones walked into the classroom and immediately began lecturing about different energy levels in the environment. Sydney scribbled in her notebook while Henry typed on his computer. He hadn't taken notes in a long time so she knew he was feeling better—at least a little bit. Every few minutes, Coen would scribble a love note on her paper. She smiled when she read it then covered it with her hand so Henry wouldn't see it. Henry was accepting and supportive of her relationship with Coen, but she didn't want to make him feel worse than he already did.

Sitting next to Coen made the electricity spark like it always did. It was almost too distracting. Even in jeans and a shirt, he looked absolutely delicious. After she told him about her horrific past, she really did feel better. Now she felt an even stronger connection to him than she already did. If she was sure of nothing else, she was sure of the love they shared for one another. Never in her life had she trusted and relied on someone so much. He was everything to her—even more than everything. Now she just wanted to go home and be alone with him, talking and making love. Her need for him wasn't lustful, although she did feel the burn between her legs when she thought about him. She just needed that connection whenever possible. She felt addicted to sex—addicted to Coen.

When the class was over, Coen walked Sydney to her next period. Henry walked alongside them. He didn't reach for her hand, which made Sydney equally relieved and sad. His hands were in his pockets but his shoulder was touching her, being affectionate in some way. She was grateful that Coen still liked Henry even though he kissed her, but they both knew Henry respected and loved her. He would never touch her like that again. Also, it was obvious how guilty he felt about the whole thing.

When they reached the lecture hall, Coen nodded to her. "Have fun."

She sighed. "I'll try."

"I'll see you at lunch," he said as he walked away.

Sydney stared at his ass as he walked down the hallway before she went inside, trying to push her fantasies to the back of her mind. Henry and Sydney sat down in their usual seats in the back. Henry typed on his computer while Sydney tried to focus on the lecture. Her mind kept wandering to Coen until it started to annoy her. If he was all she ever thought about, she was going to fail all her classes. She imagined him lying on top of her, moving into her slowly while he looked in her eyes. He stretched her so much that it blasted her mind with pleasure. She shook the thought away because the area between her legs was starting to burn.

When the class finally ended, she and Henry walked to the cafeteria and sat at their usual table. Nancy was already sitting there and she was about to mention her relationship with Coen when a tofu salad was placed in front of her.

Coen smiled at her as he took his seat. "The dressing is on the side," he said as he bit into his sandwich.

She thought it was sweet that he brought her lunch. She liked being independent, never allowing people to do things for her, but she liked it when Coen did it. For the first time, she loved being taken care of. She didn't feel weak or pathetic, just loved. "Thank you."

48

He opened his textbook and started to flip through the pages. Henry was typing on his computer, organizing his notes, and Nancy looked at her phone. Sydney never mentioned or even acted like she recognized Nancy's attraction to Coen because she just wanted to forget about it. Her friend had no idea that she and Coen were together. She couldn't be mad about it.

Her first instinct was to place her hand on Coen's thigh like she did when they drove in his car, but she knew she couldn't do that with Henry sitting across from her. She would just have to be patient.

Everything seemed calm until Sydney looked across the room and saw Audrey, Coen's psycho ex, glaring at her with so much hate she thought she would explode. Sydney sighed, annoyed that this was going to be an issue. Obviously, word had traveled that she and Coen were together. Audrey wasn't happy about it.

When Audrey started marching toward their table, Sydney tried to calm herself before the battle started. She knew she couldn't hurt her even though she wanted to. Fighting was unacceptable on campus. She could lose her scholarship and her admission to the university because of it.

When Audrey reached the table, Coen stood up and moved forward, keeping Audrey away from Sydney, protecting her with his body. Sydney sighed in relief when he did that.

Coen crossed his arms over his chest. "Can I help you?"

She glared at him. "I heard that man-looking whore was your girlfriend. Is that true?"

"I don't know what you're talking about."

Sydney raised an eyebrow, unsure what he was playing. Henry closed his laptop then glared at Audrey, obviously furious that she just insulted Sydney like that. Nancy looked like she was going to punch her.

"I have an absolutely gorgeous girlfriend named Sydney, who I'm madly in love with. Perhaps you are confused."

"She's totally hideous," she snapped, putting her hands on her hips. "How could you date her?"

"You're hideous. She makes you look like the ass of a skunk."

Nancy chuckled when he said that.

Audrey glanced at her then returned her look to Coen. "You didn't seem to think that when you were fucking me."

Sydney wanted to gag at the thought. She hated imagining him with anyone else.

He placed his hand on her arm then gently pushed her back. "Fuck off and leave me alone. We're never getting back together. I don't want you."

"I don't think so. I'm not going to let you settle for this butch dyke."

He stuck his face close to hers. "Go fuck yourself. Leave me and Sydney alone. I mean it."

"No."

He grabbed his soda and poured it over her head. She gasped as the sticky syrup leaked into her hair and skin.

"Yes!" Nancy shouted.

Henry laughed hysterically, clapping his hands together. "You look like shit."

"Sorry," Coen said as he looked at her. "I must have tripped."

She slapped him across the face as hard as she could before she marched off. Furious, Sydney stood up and was about to chase after her. She refused to let anyone hit Coen like that.

"Baby, it's okay. Sit down."

She looked at him then lowered herself back to her seat.

He sat down and sighed. "I apologize for that."

"That was totally awesome," Nancy said. "I'm so glad I got to watch."

"It was the second most satisfying thing you could have done, besides slapping that whore as hard as possible," Henry said. "That bitch got what was coming to her."

Coen looked at Sydney. "You okay?"

She nodded. "I wish you hadn't done that."

"She wouldn't stop. I had to. She has to know that I won't tolerate her behavior."

"That was still really mean."

"And her saying all those insults about you weren't?"

"They're just words. You tell me how beautiful I am all the time. Her opinion holds no value to me."

He sighed. "You are a much better person than I'll ever be."

"I think we should just ignore her from now on. She can say whatever she wants. It says more about her than it does about us."

"Okay," he said as he looked at her. "But if she ever tries to touch you, you better beat the shit out of her."

"I can't do that."

"Why?"

"Because it's a crime."

"Not if it's self-defense."

"I refuse to hit someone unless I fear for my life."

"Well, it would never come to that."

"I hope not."

"It won't. I'll make sure she doesn't bother you—without pouring stuff on her."

"Thank you."

"She'll probably just keep bugging me anyway, trying to seduce me and shit."

Nancy leaned forward. "I think we should blindfold her and jump her. That should do the trick. Scare the shit out of her."

"That's not funny," Sydney said.

She rolled her eyes. "You're no fun."

Henry opened his laptop again. "She won't bother you, Syd. Both Coen and me have your back. Don't worry about it."

She smiled. "Okay."

After they finished their afternoon classes, Henry and Sydney walked to the parking lot.

"You wanna hang out today?" she asked.

"Uh, I guess."

"We can swim in the ocean."

"No," he said quickly.

"Why?"

He was quiet for a moment. "I don't like seeing you in a swimsuit."

"Oh." The meaning dawned on her. "Oh."

"Yeah."

"I can wear something else."

"That would be appreciated."

"So you still want to hang out with me?"

"Yeah. But I need to get ready for my date right afterwards."

"Where are you taking her?"

"The Tiki Diner."

"That's not very romantic."

"Well, I don't want to be too serious. We're just hanging out. I'm not going to kiss her or anything."

"I guess."

"So you want me to come now?"

She looked over his shoulder and saw Coen approaching them. His backpack was on his shoulder and his shirt was pulled against his chest, showing the lines of his pectoral muscles. When she imagined him naked, she felt the moisture start to seep from between her legs. "How about in an hour?"

"Okay."

"Hour and a half," she added quickly.

"That works too. I'll see you then." He turned away and walked to his car.

Coen reached her but didn't touch her because Henry was still in their vicinity. "Hey."

"Come over," she said bluntly.

"Well, I have to go to work soon and do some studying."

"Just a quickie."

His eyes lit up. "You get straight to the point."

"I don't care. I want you."

"Let's do it."

"Henry is coming over in an hour so you need to be gone by then."

"What are you guys doing?"

"Swimming."

"What will you be wearing?"

"Long shorts and a swim shirt."

He nodded his head in approval. "No reason to torture the guy." He kissed her on the forehead. "I'll head over now."

"Okay," she said as she climbed into her Jeep. After she left the parking lot, she kept thinking about being with him and just the thought made her want to explode. She went to the clinic that morning and got her pills but they still had to wait a week before it was safe. When she parked her car, Coen pulled up beside her.

Without speaking, they both walked into the house then shut the door behind them.

He pushed her against the wall and pressed his mouth against hers, slipping his tongue in with no preamble whatsoever. She moaned and slipped her hands under his shirt, feeling the grooves of his stomach. His hands moved under her bra and squeezed her tits while he pressed his hard cock against her thigh.

She was ready to go, had been ready all day, so she pulled him toward her bedroom, kissing the entire way.

They bumped into the walls and knocked down a few picture frames but neither one seemed to notice. When they got into her bedroom, his pants were around his ankles and her shirt and bra were gone.

She ripped off the rest of his clothes without being gentle, just kissing his lips or his body. His free cock rubbed against her as she moved, liquid escaping from the tip. When he pulled off her pants and underwear, he kneeled and kissed the area between her legs. She yelped as if she was in pain. Her skin was blazing with heat and just the slightest touch made her tremble.

He guided her to the bed and climbed on top of her. She grabbed the condom and opened it while he adjusted her legs, pulling her hips toward him. His hips pulsed as she slid the condom onto his large size. He was breathing heavily, panting as the latex enclosed him completely. She pulled the tip up so he had plenty of room to come. They both knew how the other wanted it. It was unnecessary to ask.

He slipped inside her with a single movement, reaching her all the way into the back.

"Yeah," she said into his mouth.

He immediately started to fuck her hard. When she scratched him with her nails, almost drawing blood, he knew she loved how fast he was pounding into her. The headboard slammed into the wall, denting the wood, but Coen didn't care. All he cared about was feeling his dick slide in and out while he looked at her. He had too many fuckings to count, but being with Sydney was the most satisfying experience he ever had. His aggressive need to fuck without thinking was met, but his heart was numbed in happiness when he made love to her. She gave him everything he ever needed. He tried to satisfy her but she never seemed to be sated. When he gave everything to her, she still wanted more. There was nothing left to give but he kept trying to fulfill her need for him. A girl had never wanted him this bad before. It was like he was air that she needed to breathe.

Her tits rocked back and forth and he moved inside her as quickly as he could. Her legs wrapped around him, holding him tightly as she screamed for him, moaning his name incoherently. His skin became tender as his dick twitched in anticipation of his orgasm. She made it so hard not to come because she felt so good. Hearing her beg him to fuck her even harder just made it more challenging.

When she grabbed his ass and pulled him deeper inside of her, fucking him from below as hard as he fucked her from above, he knew she was about to come. Her chest turned red and her nipples hardened as her breathing became loud gasps. The pleasure was so much that she couldn't bottle it all inside. Her nails dug into his skin as she exploded. Coen kept up the pace to make her moment last as long as possible. When he felt the increased moisture surround him, he knew she was done. Her head lay back as she regained her composure, still breathing like she ran a marathon. The sweat trickled to the area between her beasts, forming a small pool. Unable to stop himself, he licked it away.

She grabbed him then turned him over, straddling him in one fluid motion. She started to ride him while his hips relaxed. When he grabbed her waist, she pulled his hands off and pinned them behind his head. She rode him slowly, taking him all the way in then pulling him out. He moaned as he lay there, feeling her do all the work. When she leaned over, her tits were directly in his face. Strands of her hair fell on his shoulder as she moved on top of him. She looked too beautiful to last long. After a few strokes, he felt his orgasm start. His breathing increased and gasps escaped his lips.

She suddenly stopped until the tingling disappeared.

He moaned in frustration.

She inserted him again and started to ride him the same way, bringing him right back to the point of release. When he felt the formation inside his balls, she pulled him out again.

"Stop," he begged. "Let me come."

She kissed his forehead. "You will." She sheathed him again.

In a matter of seconds, he was ready to come again. The pleasure started to prickle his skin. He was almost there. Just a few more strokes and he would finally come. "Please."

She moved over him, making every stroke as tantalizing as the last. "Come."

His hips bucked forward as the strongest orgasm he ever had in his life shot through him, electrifying every single inch of his skin. He even felt it in his nose and his toes. Gasping for breath, he leaned his head back as the come shot out of him, filling the entire tip of the condom. His was shaking, unable to hold all the pleasure he was feeling. He was breathless, winded as he lay still, looking up at her.

She smiled at him then rubbed her nose against his.

"Mwah."

"I love you too." She ran her fingers through his hair then rubbed his chest.

"Holy fucking shit."

"So you liked that, I take it?"

"Fuck yeah. I've never come harder in my life."

She leaned back then pulled him out before she pulled the used condom off then threw it in the trash.

"When can we stop using condoms?"

"One week."

"It's gonna take me a while before I can build up my tolerance."

"Then we have to have lots of sex."

"Yeah."

She snuggled next to him. "I want to fuck again before you go."

"I don't think I can. That took everything out of me."

She pouted. "I need something to hold me over until tonight."

"What's tonight?"

"You're coming over, right?"

"To visit or just to fuck?"

"You can do either, but I was referring to the fucking. And can we do it before school every morning?"

He stared at her, incredulous. "So three times a day, every day?"

"Exactly."

"Damn. I thought orgasms were supposed to satisfy you, not spur you on."

"You don't have to if you don't want to," she said sadly.

"It's not that," he said quickly. "I've just never been with a woman who's wanted me so much."

"I'm in love with you. I need you inside me all the time."

"I don't know how I got so lucky," he said as he climbed on top of her, pulling her hips to him. Without another word, he pressed his lips against her clitoris and kissed it gently. Her fingers fisted his hair as he licked her, circling the nub with precision. He hated giving head and hardly ever did with other girls, but he enjoyed doing it with Sydney. The joy on her face as he made her legs shake made him harder than a nail. When he slipped his tongue inside her, she started to moan even louder. His dick twitched as it sprang to life. When he thought he couldn't get aroused again, she always proved him wrong. Her moans and shouts made him pull away. He grabbed another condom and slipped it on.

She eyed his cock as he prepared himself to enter. He moved back on top of her and pressed his forehead against hers. He was back inside her instantly, exactly where he belonged. She grabbed his shoulders and tensed as he moved inside her. Her breaths filled his mouth as he rocked her gently.

When she gripped his upper arms, he knew she was about to explode. She was already charged so much she thought her body would give out because it was unable to handle all the emotions she felt.

Coen kissed the skin over her heart then returned to her. "You're the love of my life."

She started panting, gripping him harder. "Coen."

"Come with me."

She gripped his back and forced him further inside her, ready to unleash. When her mouth flew open with a scream, he let himself go, imagining he was filling her, not the inside of the latex. She repeated his name as she rode her high. When Coen was finished, his body shook in exhaustion. Lovemaking always took more out of him than fucking because his heart bled so much. He gave himself to her entirely, letting her envelope him completely. He gave Audrey a part of his heart, but he gave Sydney the entire thing, plus the rest of him. Without her, he was nothing.

She lay back and held him to her, calming down from her high as he tried to catch his breath. He kissed her on the forehead.

"You knock the wind out of me every time."

"Oops."

He rubbed his nose against hers. "I've never loved anyone the way I love you."

"I know," she whispered. "I can tell."

"And I can tell you feel the same way."

"More than you will ever know."

He looked at the clock and sighed. "I should go."

She groaned. "I don't want you to."

"Do you really want Henry to see me? I think it's pretty obvious what we were just doing."

"You're right."

He pulled on his clothes then fixed his hair in the mirror.

She pulled on her swimsuit then her board shorts and a shirt. He nodded in approval when he saw her. "Coen, can I ask you something?"

"You don't need to ask. You are always welcome to ask me whatever you want."

"Does Audrey still come to you for training?"

"No. Ever since I told my boss she lied on her application, she isn't allowed to work with a personal trainer."

"Well, does she still bother you?"

"I thought you didn't want to know?"

"I changed my mind," she said quietly.

"She's come to my apartment a few times, wearing a jacket with nothing underneath. The only reason I know that is because she flashed me before I slammed the door in her face. She still calls me randomly, sometimes it's late at night. She still sends me naked—"

"Okay. Stop."

He looked at her. "I'm sorry. You told me you wanted to know."

"I want her to leave you alone."

"I do too, baby. She'll stop bothering me eventually. After we've been together for a while, she'll give up and find someone else."

"Maybe I can hook Aaron up with her."

"Well, they probably already slept together. I doubt he wants to repeat that."

"Well, I'm desperate."

He wrapped his arms around her waist, pressing his forehead against hers. "You never have to worry about something happening between us—ever. I don't even drink or eat around her because I can't trust her. I'm yours."

She sighed. "I trust you. I'm just getting tired of it."

"I understand. It would drive me crazy too."

She said nothing.

"You could beat her up and scare her off," he said with a smile. "Claim your territory."

"Violence solves nothing."

"Just this one time."

"No. That isn't why I trained."

"So you learned to fight so you could kill your stepfather and stepbrother?"

"No. I did it to defend myself. When I see them again, they won't be able to touch me."

"*If* you see them again—which will be never. I refuse to let that happen."

She said nothing.

He released his hold then walked to the front door. "I should get going."

"You're coming back, right?"

"That depends. Can I have a drawer?"

She smiled. "You can have as many drawers as you want."

"And can I leave my stuff here?"

"Of course."

"Then, yes, I'll be back."

"Please sleep with me."

He kissed her forehead. "I'll sleep with you every night, okay?"

She breathed a sigh of relief. "I'm sorry. I just don't have nightmares when I'm with you. I don't mean to be so needy."

"I love it when you're needy."

"You do?"

"Yes. Don't ever worry about that."

"Thank you."

"Now I really have to go. We're cutting it close."

"Okay." She gave him a quick kiss and he walked out the door, jumping into his car. A few minutes after he left, Henry pulled into the driveway. That was good timing.

"Hey," he said as he approached her. "Ready to hit the beach?"

"Yep," she said as she threw him a towel.

They walked down to the coast and immediately jumped in the water, feeling the sand from the ocean floor.

"Are we swimming with whales today?"

"I haven't seen them lately," she said sadly.

"Does Coen know you're crazy?"

She smiled. "Yes."

"Poor guy."

She splashed water into his face and he splashed it back. "So, do you know what your moves are tonight?"

"Moves? I don't have moves."

"Then what do you do?"

He shrugged. "I kiss a girl if I like her. I ask to take her back to my place if I want to fuck her and never call her again."

She was quiet for a moment. "I can't see you doing that."

"That's because I'm always a nice guy around you. Also, I hardly ever do that, and when I do, she's perfectly aware of my intentions. It surprises me how many women are interested in casual sex."

"That surprises me too."

He floated on the water, riding the waves. "So, how are things between you and Coen?"

"Good."

"Give me more than that, Syd."

"What do you mean?"

"You can talk to me about him like you would talk about anyone else. You don't have to hold back because of my feelings."

She looked at the ocean floor and saw a shell. She moved away so she wouldn't crush it. "I don't want to hurt you."

"I can't hurt more than I already am."

Her face contorted in a grimace.

He sighed then swam over to her. "This is a good thing. I'm moving on without any regrets. I want us to be back to normal. Obviously, it's going to be awkward for a while, but if we just act normal then it will be normal eventually."

"Are you sure?"

"I care about you and what happens in your life. You don't have to hide anything from me. And I don't care if you're affectionate with Coen at school. You don't have to tone it down for me."

"I can't believe how selfless you are."

He shook his head. "That couldn't be further from the truth. I want you to hurt me because it will help me move on. Just be normal—please."

"Okay."

"Thank you. So, let's do this."

She sighed. "I've never loved anyone the way I love him."

"Is he the one?"

"Definitely."

He looked up at the sky as he floated. The sun was starting to set but they still had some sunlight left. "Does he know how you feel?"

"Yes. He feels the same way."

"Have you guys had sex?"

"Yeah."

"Is he better than Aaron?"

"Better than anyone." His face appeared stoic like he wasn't in pain. Perhaps they would return to normal eventually.

"I never would have expected it to be him."

"Neither did I. He's one of the greatest men I know."

"What's his tattoo?"

"His dog died. He wanted something to remember him by."

Henry nodded.

"So, when was the last time you had sex?" Sydney asked.

He laughed. "I don't remember discussing this before."

"Well, we are friends, right?"

"A few months ago."

"Do you want to score tonight?"

"Not really. I'm just not there right now."

"You're going to find someone that you love way more than you ever loved me."

He said nothing for a long time. "I know, Syd."

"And if things were different, I would have given you a chance."

He groaned, covering his face with his hands. "Please stop."

"What?"

"That just makes me feel worse. If I had made a move before Coen, you could have been mine. Now I feel nothing but regret."

"But I don't think I wouldn't have fallen in love with you, Henry. We are just too good of friends. So no, you don't have to regret anything."

"That makes it a little better."

"I'm glad."

He floated in the ocean then dived under the water. When he surfaced, he was holding a crab shell. "Look at this little guy."

She swam to him then held the small crab in her hands. "He's cute."

"We should paint his shell."

"No. Then he'll be more visible to predators."

"Or they'll think he's poisonous and badass."

She smiled. "He's beautiful."

"No. Badass crabs aren't cute and beautiful. They are ferocious and aggressive."

The crab walked across her palm at the speed of a snail.

She raised an eyebrow. "He seems pretty harmless to me."

"Well, the smaller crabs should be afraid."

She touched the outside of the shell with her finger then returned it to the water. "I've always wanted to see seahorses in the wild. I've only found a few and they usually swim away."

"They are pretty hard to see." He looked around in the water then glided across the surface, his head down. There were a few rocks and underwater plants they could hide in. Without moving his head, he waved her over. Excited, she swam to him then glided beside him. Near the plants were two seahorses sitting on the stems of the seaweed. Their tails were wrapped around one another. She stared at them for a long time until she needed to breathe. She lifted her head then took a deep breath before she ducked back underwater. One of them looked bigger than the other, swollen in the belly. They had tiny fins on their heads that helped them move or sit up straight. Their tails remained tangled together, locked like they were holding hands. It was one of the most beautiful things she'd ever seen. When Henry lifted his head for a deep breath, the movement scared them and they scurried off.

"That was amazing," she said.

"I like how their tails were locked together."

"They're so cute."

"You think everything is cute."

"I don't deny that."

He smiled. "It's one of the reasons why I love you." She looked at him, her smile fading. "As a friend," he added quickly. "You are kind to those who don't deserve it and you would give your life to protect an innocent creature. It's very honorable."

"I'm glad you don't think I'm crazy."

"I never said that. You're definitely insane. But I like it."

She smiled again.

"Coen is a very lucky guy."

"Henry."

He looked up at the sky again. "I should get going. I have to wash the smell of salt from my skin."

"You should sleep with her," she blurted.

"What? Why?"

"It will help."

He walked up to the beach then dried himself off with a towel. "Not to make you uncomfortable, but I can't do that because all I'll think about is you."

She said nothing.

They walked back to the house and Henry grabbed his clothes from the porch.

"I'll see you later," he said as he walked away.

She waved to him. "Bye."

He disappeared from the driveway. He didn't hug her anymore. It was something she noticed immediately. She was glad it wasn't an issue anymore. It would just make everything awkward. Before she went inside, Coen's car pulled up. She smiled when she saw him. She sprinted toward him, smiling the entire way, until she jumped in his arms and wrapped her legs around his waist.

"It's only been a few hours," he said with a laugh. He walked toward the house while he carried her then entered through the front door.

"I know. It was agonizing."

He laughed. "I like it when you do that."

"What?"

"Run at me, like I'm the only thing in the world that matters to you."

"You are the only thing that matters."

"I know that isn't true," he said as he placed her on the couch. "So, how was it with Henry?"

She shrugged. "We're getting there."

"I hate to be blunt but it will never be the same between you. You were never friends to begin with."

"Yes, we were," she said defensively.

"On your part, yes. On his part, no. It will never be what it once was."

She looked down at her hands and stared at them.

"I say this so you don't get your expectations up. You can be close friends again but the relationship will be different. Don't try to recreate what you had. Try to become different than you used to be."

She nodded. "You're right, Coen."

"I know I am."

"We talked about you."

"And what was said?"

"I told him that we've had sex and that I love you."

"And his response?"

"He seemed to be okay with it. I asked about his personal life. He's slept around but no one interesting has caught his eye."

"Does he want to get laid tonight?"

"He said no."

"He'll get there eventually."

Her eyes lit up in delight. "We saw seahorses."

"Really? That's so cool."

"There were two of them. Their tails were wrapped around each other. It was so adorable."

He wrapped his finger around hers. "You know seahorses mate for life, right?"

"I know. That's so amazing."

"Yeah." His pinky was wrapped around hers. "Just like humans."

She smiled. "Do you want to be my seahorse?"

"I assumed that I was already."

Her eyes watered. "That's the sweetest thing I've ever heard."

He rubbed his nose against hers. "And my seahorse is the most beautiful one in the world. I'm just glad that you still have to carry the babies."

"That isn't fair."

"You'll look hot being pregnant. I could never pull that off."

"I'll be fat and round."

"Only your stomach will be. And it will be so sexy."

"I don't know about that."

"I do."

She rolled her eyes. "Let's go to bed."

"What? I don't get dinner or attention? You just want to go straight to home base?"

"There're pancakes and eggs for days in the refrigerator."

"Wanna go out to dinner?"

"No. I want to stay home with you."

"Whatever my seahorse wants."

She pulled him to his feet and dragged him to the bedroom.

6

Sydney pulled into the parking lot and grabbed her backpack from the backseat. When she jumped down, she saw Audrey looking at her from the sidewalk. After she smiled at her, she walked toward the science building. Sydney's blood turned ice cold. It was just a smile but it was definitely frightening. She was grateful she couldn't read that bitch's mind.

"You okay?" Henry asked as he approached her.

"Uh, yeah."

"Did Audrey say something to you?"

"She smiled at me."

He raised an eyebrow. "Is that a good thing?"

"In the girl world, that's a death sentence."

He shook his head. "I'll never understand women."

"Neither will I."

Coen slid his arm around her waist and kissed her on the forehead. "Hey, seahorse."

"Hey." It was a nickname that stuck. He called her that almost every day. She loved hearing it because it was the sweetest thing she ever heard. They were life partners, mates for life—at least that's what they wanted. Henry didn't comment on the odd nickname.

The past month seemed to pass by like a blur. She spent almost all of her time with Coen exclusively. She felt guilty for bailing on her friends and skipping a lot of parties, but would much rather spend time with Coen, seeing him naked, than be around a bunch of people that she felt indifferent to. Audrey hadn't bothered her again, but after that smile, she suspected something horrible would happen.

Coen kept his arm around her waist as he walked her to the building. Henry kept his hands in his pockets as he walked beside them. He seemed to accept Sydney's relationship with Coen more as the days wore on. He told her he was fooling around with the same girl for a while. That had to be good news. He obviously wasn't in love with her, but at least he was starting to picture himself with other women.

The fire between Coen and Sydney didn't seem to die down even though they had sex more than any normal couple should, but it increased even more. Even when she was on her period, they both had to have it. Oral sex wouldn't suffice for either one of them. When they stopped using condoms, Coen couldn't last as long as he normally did, so they spent an entire weekend doing nothing else but sex. By Monday, his threshold had increased substantially.

The more time she spent with him, the more in love she became. She wondered how she had lived without him for so long. He was perfect for her in every way, her other half, her seahorse. He didn't mention her horrific past, but she didn't think about it as often anymore. And she hadn't had a single nightmare since he started to sleep at her place every night. She felt whole and complete for the first time in her life, like she belonged somewhere. She had a family—Coen was her family.

Coen looked at her sundress. "You look lovely today."

"Thank you. I know this is your favorite."

"They are all my favorite," he said as he dug his fingers into her side, feeling the fabric.

When they entered the building, they walked up the stairs until they reached the hallway where their zoology class was located. When Audrey and two other girls walked past them, she knew something horrible was about to happen.

They passed without incident. But it didn't slow her beating heart in any way.

When Henry opened the door for her, she felt hot syrup pour on top of her head, streaming past her eyes and down her clothes. It was so sticky and thick that she couldn't breathe. She had to rip open a hole in the goo so she could suck in a breath. Henry shut the door and turned around, glaring at Audrey, who was laughing hysterically. Her two friends laughed along with her.

Coen pushed her against the wall, making her laugh stop immediately. "What the hell is wrong with you?"

Henry pulled Sydney's backpack off so she wouldn't ruin her belongings or her phone. He took her in the bathroom and helped put her head under the sink. Henry helped her wash the syrup from her hair but it hardened as soon it touched her strands.

Sydney tried not to cry because she knew it was stupid to cry. She choked it back and concentrated on cleaning herself up. Coen was still in the hallway and she hoped he finally convinced Audrey to start acting like an adult. She had never been bullied in school before. Only when she got home did the violence start. This was nothing compared to that. She kept reminding herself that she would never feel that pain again. This was just a stupid prank that hardly anyone saw.

Coen burst through the doors then came over to her, helping them both wash the goop out of her hair. "You okay?" he asked as he placed his hand on her back.

"I'm fine," she said with a strong voice.

"I'm so sorry."

"It's not your fault, Coen."

Henry stared at him with a hard expression. "Did you get her to apologize or agree to stop?"

He was quiet for a moment. "No."

"I'll do it, then," he said quickly. "Chivalry is dead. She fucks with my friend, then I fuck with her."

Sydney grabbed his arm. "Let it go."

"No," he snapped.

"It's not worth it."

"She's just going to keep doing this to you, Syd."

"No, she won't. She'll stop."

Coen rubbed her back. "I already threatened to kill her. That should be enough for now."

She turned off the sink then squeezed the water from her hair. It was still a little sticky but she managed to get rid of most of it.

"You wanna go home and shower?" Coen asked.

"No. I'm not skipping class because of that bitch. She'll have to do worse than that. I'm not obsessed with my hair like they are."

Even though it was inappropriate, Coen smiled. "You're amazing."

"You already said that."

"You keep surprising me."

She grabbed some towels and dried her face and her neck. She stuck her head under a hand dryer and dried the damp strands of hair. She rubbed it with her fingers then straightened out the knots. "Good as new." She walked out with the two boys following behind her. They went to class and listened to the lecture then took their quiz at the end of the period.

After their next class, they went to the cafeteria. When they sat down, Sydney spotted Audrey glaring at her from her table. She smiled at her then grabbed Coen and kissed him hard on the mouth, wanting to piss her off as much as possible. When she broke their kiss, Audrey was even angrier.

"What was that for?" Coen asked, his lips still slightly open.

"Audrey."

"Wait. What?"

"She was staring at us. I wanted to give her a reason to stare."

Henry glanced at her. "If she tries anything, I don't care what happens to me. I'm going to teach her a lesson and make the bitch cry."

Sydney grabbed his hand. "Promise me you won't."

"No," he said as he pulled away.

"Henry," she pressed.

Coen looked at him. "She's right. Let it go. She's my problem. I'll handle her."

"Then nothing better happen to Sydney again," he snapped, his eyes wide with venom. "If you can't take care of her, I will."

Sydney was shocked by the anger in his voice. Henry never got angry. And she'd never seen him challenge Coen like that, blatantly saying he was better for her than he was.

"I got it under control," Coen snapped.

"It doesn't seem like it."

"I didn't know she was going to dump a tub of syrup on Sydney! She snuck up on you too."

"But Sydney isn't my girlfriend. If she were, believe me, I would have noticed."

Sydney didn't like where this conversation was headed at all. "Knock it off—both of you."

Coen glared at him.

"I mean it," she said. "It's no one's fault. I'm fine."

Henry looked away. "It better stay that way." He looked at Audrey again. "She's twice your height."

"That won't be a problem," she said. She hadn't told Henry about the level of her training so she didn't want to bring it up now. It was better left unsaid.

Coen stood up. "I'll go deal with her right now."

"Just leave it alone," she said but Coen was already halfway across the room.

"This is total bullshit," Henry said. "You're being harassed. Go to the dean or something."

"We aren't in high school anymore. It doesn't work like that."

"Then go to the police."

"I'm not doing that either. It stays between us."

"Why?"

"Because I'm not a pussy," she snapped.

Henry raised an eyebrow, shocked by her expression.

"I can handle her. Don't worry about it."

Coen returned a few minutes later and dropped into his seat with a heavy sigh.

"So?" she asked.

"She said she won't stop until I break up with you."

"And what did you say?"

"That I don't negotiate with terrorists."

Sydney chuckled. "That's a perfect description of what she is."

Nancy shook her head. "I seriously want to beat this bitch's face in. I fucking hate her."

"Don't worry about her," Coen said. "I'll watch out for her."

"And I'll walk you to your classes when Coen can't," Henry said.

"I appreciate it but you don't need to do that—either of you. I can take care of myself. She just caught me off guard today."

"I know you can but it still gives me peace of mind when I walk you," Coen said.

"Coen, no. I refuse to live in fear."

He stared at her, silently communicating with her. Her past was something she struggled with her whole life. He knew this wasn't any different. She wanted to fight her own battles and stand on her own two feet. He couldn't take that away from her. "Okay."

"Thank you."

Nancy glanced at Audrey then turned back to Sydney. "When's the trip out to sea?"

"In a few days," she said with a smile.

"Are you excited?" she asked.

"And nervous. I just hope I don't piss him off. People who have a PhD are always weird."

"Don't you want to get your PhD?" Coen asked with a laugh.

"Yeah," Sydney said. "I admit it. I'm weird."

"Are you missing school?" Nancy asked.

"Just Friday. When I told my teachers what it was for, they were supportive."

"Cool," Henry said. "Just be careful. You won't be by the coast anymore."

"I know." She grabbed her bag and placed it over her shoulder. "I'll see you guys later." She kissed Coen then walked to her English class. Even though science was her passion, she still loved reading and writing. She wrote a few poems and short stories but never showed them to anyone. When her class was over, she left the building and walked down the sidewalk, which winded through the campus. Most of the students were gone for the day. The sun shined overhead and made her sweat as she walked. She was excited to go home and lie in bed with Coen, forgetting about the horrific day she just had.

"Hey."

Sydney looked up from her feet and saw Audrey standing in front of her. "What?" she snapped.

"You're awfully brave for being around three girls that want nothing more than to smash your face against the concrete until it splits in half."

"Are we juniors in high school or juniors in college?" She stepped around Audrey with her back straight.

Audrey yanked her bag off then threw it on the ground.

Sydney was thankful her computer wasn't in there, but her phone was. She hoped it wasn't broken.

"Break up with Coen and it will make your life a lot easier."

"Why? He wouldn't date you anyway."

"Yes, he would."

"He loves me, not you."

"He'll forget about all of that once he's inside of me."

"Rape—what a turn on."

"It won't be rape," she said as she glared at her.

"No. I love him and he loves me. You can break my face but it wouldn't change a thing. He'll still choose me over you."

"Really?" she asked with a smile. She pulled out her phone then pressed a button. A video started to play. It showed Coen on top of her, thrusting inside of her. She knew it was him by his tattoo. The sight broke her heart but she hid the pain on her face, not giving her any satisfaction. "That was from yesterday."

"He was with me all day."

"And what about all night?"

"He slept in my arms."

She shook her head. "Poor girl. He's been chasing tail this whole time. You actually thought he cared for you? He's been sleeping around since you got together."

"Liar."

"I wish I were."

Sydney reached for her bag but Audrey stepped on it. "Move," she snapped.

"No."

Sydney wanted to hit her, but she had to wait for her to throw the first punch. If not, it wouldn't be self-defense. "Coen told me I was the best he ever had."

"He said the same thing to me."

"Another lie."

"Break up with him."

"I would rather die."

Audrey removed her foot then stepped closer to her. Sydney didn't back down. She waited for her to make a move, slamming her fist against her face. She wanted it more than anything. As soon as she did, Sydney would put this bitch in her place.

"Sydney!"

Sydney sighed in frustration. She wanted this fight to happen.

Coen ran toward her with Henry right behind her. He pushed Audrey out of the way then wrapped his arms around her. "Are you okay?"

"I'm fine," she said as she pushed him out of the way. She stepped up to Audrey. "Do you have anything else to say to me?"

"Do what I say, bitch. You'll regret it if you don't."

"No. Coen is mine. It's not my fault that you couldn't keep your legs closed." She grabbed her bag then placed it over her shoulder. Audrey glared at her for a moment before she walked away.

Coen pressed his face against Audrey's. "You touch her, I'll kill you." He glared at her then walked next to Sydney with Henry on her other side.

Henry looked concerned. "Are you okay?"

"I'm fine," she said as she walked forward.

"Did she hurt you?" Coen asked.

"She could never."

"Maybe we should talk to someone," Coen said. "She's actually stalking you."

"No," she said. "I can handle it."

"I hate this. I'm so sorry," he said as he squeezed her hand. "I understand if you don't want to be with me anymore."

"That would never happen, Coen. I love you. I'll fight forever for you."

He sighed. "I don't deserve you."

Henry didn't comment on their affectionate words. They walked across the campus until they reached the parking lot. Both men walked her directly to her car. When they saw her Jeep in the parking lot, they all stopped.

Sydney dropped her bag when she looked at her car. Mustard was smeared everywhere, spelling out "whore" and "nasty cunt." She wiped the mustard away but it was too late. It already stained the paint. She moved to the seats and saw that more of the yellow liquid was sprayed all over her seats. Everything was demolished—ruined. She kept her tears in the back of her throat. "This was my dad's."

Coen covered his face and sighed. "Fuck."

Henry placed his hand on her shoulder but said nothing.

She stared at the car, one of the few things she had left of her father, and felt a tear roll down her cheek.

The Jeep wouldn't start, so Coen popped the engine with Henry and looked inside. Sydney sat against the tire and clutched her stomach, depressed that her car was completely destroyed. It was vandalized and now it didn't even work. Even if it did start, she couldn't drive around town with such obscene words painted on the surface. She wished she could call the police and report the damages but it was pointless. She had no proof that Audrey was the culprit and her insurance payment would increase because of the incident. It wasn't worth it. She would have to strip it for parts and save some money to buy a car.

"I think they squirted mustard in the oil container," Coen said as he wiped the sweat from his forehead.

"Let me see," Henry said. He peered inside. "Probably."

"We need to get this back to the shack so no one sees it. I'll tow it with my truck. Help me with the cables."

"Yeah," Henry said as he followed him.

They hooked up the cables then helped Sydney into the passenger seat. She was too depressed to care about anything. On the ride home, Coen said nothing. His arm was hooked around her shoulder but she didn't feel it. She tried to think of other things to distract her mind from reality. How much would a new car cost? She knew Henry and Coen would give her rides whenever she needed them, but she hated asking for help.

When they pulled in the driveway, she left the car and walked into the house. She showered to get the mustard and syrup off her body then climbed into bed, too upset to stand outside and watch them discuss what to do with her useless vehicle.

Coen came in a moment later. "Baby, I'm so sorry."

"It's not your fault," she said quietly.

"Yes, it is. You don't deserve this. Maybe we should—"

"Don't even think it, Coen."

He sighed. "I'll fix your car. My dad taught me a lot about mechanics when I was younger."

"Don't bother. I wouldn't be able to drive it anyway."

"We'll figure it out."

"No. I don't want to drive it."

He leaned down and kissed her on the forehead. "Get some sleep. I'll see you when you wake up."

"Where are you going?"

"To work on your car."

"It's pointless."

"Close your eyes and relax."

She did as he asked and tried to think of different things. She felt the bed move as he stood up and left her bedroom. When she thought about letting her father down a second time, it made her want to cry. Instead, she thought about the seahorses she found in the ocean. One was yellow with spots of green and the other was brown with flecks of white. They looked so different but they were so beautiful—especially together. Her mind fell into the abyss as she thought about the magnificent creatures.

The sound of talking drifted through her window and woke her up. When she looked at the clock, she was surprised how late it was. She had been out for a long time. She got dressed then went outside.

The sides of her Jeep were missing and the engine was popped up. Coen had his sleeves rolled up and his arms were covered with black soot. A guy she had never seen before had a piece of her car frame on top of newspaper and he was painting it the same green color as the rest of the car, covering up the yellow stains. Nancy was sitting inside the car and it looked like she was hand sewing new fabric onto the seats. Laura held a coil of string and helped her tighten the patches. When she stepped closer, she saw Henry climb into the driver's seat.

"Crank it," Coen said.

Henry turned the engine and it burst to life. He hit the accelerator and they heard the engine roar.

"Shut it off," Coen shouted. He wiped his hands on his jeans then tossed the empty oil bottles into the trashcan nearby.

She stepped closer and watched them work on her car. Two other guys she didn't recognize were placing another piece of the frame back on the car. It was newly painted and shined under the street light. She couldn't believe what they were doing. Her car didn't look brand new but it looked identical to the one she had before.

Coen spotted her then approached her, a smile on his face. When he came closer to her, his grin fell. "Baby, what's wrong?"

She covered her face with her hands, trying not to cry. "You did all this?"

"Well, my friends helped." He pointed to the two men putting the covering back on the metal and the other guy using a paint sprayer on the other frame. "Two of them work at an autobody shop. Laura and Nancy came over as soon as Henry told them what happened. Henry and I managed to clean out your oil before the mustard flooded to the rest of the car."

A tear fell down her face. "I can't believe you did all this for me—everyone did this for me."

"I can."

"Thank you so much. My daddy gave this to me. I didn't know what I was going to do without it."

"I know." He didn't touch her because he was so dirty.

"I still can't believe this."

"We're family, Sydney. This is what families do."

"What about your friends? They don't even know me."

"They know I love you. That's all that matters. They would do anything for you if I asked them to."

"I have a family?"

"Yes. One that loves you very much."

After Sydney hugged everyone and thanked them for their work, they left and went to dinner near the shore. They picked a taco shop and sat outside, watching the ocean in the near distance.

Coen had his arms around her the whole time, comforting her even though she didn't need it anymore. He showered before they left so he didn't smell as bad as he did earlier, when oil and mustard was stuck in his hair.

"Thank you so much," she said to everyone again. She already said it but she was moved by the gesture. They all worked together to help her out. She didn't even need to ask them. They just did it.

Brody, Coen's friend, smiled at her. "Don't worry about it. We were glad to help."

"I've always hated that bitch, Audrey," Wayne said. "I don't know what the hell you were doing with her. I already like Sydney a million times more."

Her cheeks blushed.

"I don't know what I was thinking either, man. But I know I'm thinking clearly now." He kissed Sydney on the forehead then rubbed his nose against hers.

Scotty finished his taco then clutched the napkin in his hand. "I say we get some serious revenge on Audrey."

"No," Sydney said quickly. "She isn't worth it."

"Yes, she is," Henry said. "She could go to jail for what she did to you."

"We don't have any proof," Nancy said sadly.

"I wanna see her face when Sydney pulls in the parking lot with a car that looks practically brand new," Brody said. He had blond hair that reached his eyes slightly. He had to keep shaking it away.

"I'll tell her Coen bought it for me," Sydney said with a smile. "Maybe she'll like that."

Coen smiled. "I like it."

"I think we should all just jump her and scare the shit out of her," Nancy said. "I can guarantee that she'll leave you alone, then."

"No violence," Sydney said firmly.

Nancy rolled her eyes.

"What if we told her we were engaged?" Coen said. "She might give up and throw in the towel."

"Or she might be even bitchier," Henry said.

"What do you think, baby?" Coen asked.

"You know her better than I do." She didn't mention the video she saw of him fucking Audrey. There was no need to bring it up. It was pretty clear that he was aware that she was making a sex tape. That was his past and it was behind them both. She knew he wasn't the most moral person when it came to sex.

"I think it would work. When she sees your car is completely untarnished and you're wearing a ring on your finger, she'll realize that her lame attempts at breaking us up only made us closer."

"A ring?" she asked.

"Well, yeah. When girls get engaged, they wear rings," he said as he smiled at her.

"But then we would have to get one, smartass."

"I have one," he said.

Sydney's eyes widened. "You do?"

"My grandmother's. She gave it to me before she passed away and told me to give it to the woman I spend the rest of my life with. It's huge. It will definitely piss off Audrey."

She smiled. "Perfect."

He looked at everyone. "So just go along with it."

Everyone nodded.

Nancy smiled. "I'm so excited for tomorrow. I never thought I would look forward to going to school."

"Neither did I," Coen said.

8

When Sydney arrived at school the next day, she waited for Coen to pull in the parking lot. When he did, he marched to her and kissed her hard on the mouth before he pulled away. He reached into his pocket and withdrew the box.

"Will you marry me, seahorse?"

Her heart lurched in her throat. Even though this was all for show, it still meant something to her. She could tell by the look in his eyes that it meant something to him too. She wished it were real.

"Of course," she said as she held her hand out.

He slipped the ring on her finger and held her gaze for a moment. He tucked her hair behind her ear as he pressed his face close to hers. The diamond immediately felt heavy on her finger, weighing it down. He kissed her gently then cupped her face. Her heart raced in her chest as she felt the connection between them, binding them together. When he pulled away, she didn't want him to.

She looked down at the ring. It was a white gold band with a solitary diamond in the middle. The huge rock sparkled in the light of the sun, showing a rainbow of colors. When she looked at it, she saw Coen's eyes and her entire world. She knew she shouldn't get emotional about this because it wasn't real but she couldn't help it. She wanted Coen to be her husband someday. He already was.

When Henry approached them, he whistled. "Damn, that thing is enormous."

"Thanks," Coen said with a smile. "My grandma only wanted the best."

"Don't hurt anyone with that," Henry said.

"Well, maybe one person," she said.

"That would be awesome," Coen said. "My grandma would love that."

When they turned to the sidewalk, they saw Audrey get out of her car with her friends.

"Quick. Cup my cheek and kiss me," Coen said.

She didn't need to be told twice. She placed her left hand on his cheek, knowing the diamond would be visible, shining brighter than the sun, and there was no possibility that Audrey would miss it. It was as impossible as a sailor missing the beacon from a light house. Sydney didn't think about Audrey as she kissed Coen. Only his lips and his tongue existed in her universe. Coen held her as close as he could, practically devouring her. His hands reached across her tiny waist and felt the smooth skin. After a minute, they broke away, knowing that was plenty of time.

As expected, when they looked at Audrey, her mouth was open and emotion was in her eyes. She said nothing and didn't move. Her friends talked, their voices loud and appalled, but she still said nothing. Finally, she turned on her heel and ran away, leaving her friends behind her.

Sydney thought she would be happy at the sight but she wasn't. Not at all. She turned away from Coen and walked away.

"What are you doing?" he asked.

"I'll be right back."

Henry and Coen exchanged worried glances then followed her.

Sydney walked with them trailing behind her until she entered the science building. Since she had cried in the bathroom so many times, she knew that's exactly where Audrey was headed.

Coen grabbed her before she walked inside. "What are you doing?"

"I'll be fine," she said.

"What are you going to do?"

"Just talk." She pulled away from him then entered the bathroom. As soon as she walked inside, she heard Audrey sobbing in one of the stalls. "Audrey, it's me."

She stifled her tears for a second, startled at her presence. "Come here to gloat?"

"Not at all," she said quietly.

"Go away, you stupid bitch."

The insults washed over Sydney without taking hold. The words meant nothing. They were empty. "I'm sorry about everything."

She sniffed. "For what?"

"That you're hurt."

She said nothing for a long time. "Just go."

"I mean it. I'm sorry that I hurt you. I hope that we can move past this."

"You're really engaged to him?" she said through her tears.

"Yes."

"Then I don't want to be your friend."

"I didn't ask you to. I just want this to stop. Please stop harassing me and destroying my property. I hold no ill feelings toward you as long as you stop trying to hurt me."

She finally opened the door and looked at Sydney. She glanced at the ring then back to her face. "I didn't cheat on Cocn."

She wasn't expecting that. "What?"

"He thinks I did, but it wasn't me. I passed out at the party in the bedroom and when I woke up, two people were going at it. When I came out of the room, everyone assumed it was me. It wasn't. I swear."

"Did you tell Coen this?"

"He doesn't believe me."

"I believe you."

She wiped her tears away. "You do?"

"I know how great Coen is. Why would you want someone else?"

"Exactly," she said through her sobs.

"I'll tell him the truth—that you didn't."

"Why would you do that? Aren't you afraid that he'll leave you for me? That was the only reason we broke up."

"I'm not worried. I'm sorry your relationship ended because he didn't have all the information, but we can't just erase what we have. We're spending our lives together." Audrey looked away. "And I understand why you were so determined to win him back. It wasn't your fault."

She crossed her arms over her chest but said nothing.

"Can we move past this?"

She sighed. "I guess."

Sydney played with her fingers in her hands, standing there awkwardly. Neither of the girls looked at each other. When Audrey stopped crying, she walked to the paper towel dispenser and cleaned her makeup. When she was composed, they both left the bathroom together.

As soon as Coen saw them, his body was flexed, ready to intervene if he had to.

"It's okay," Sydney said quickly. "We talked it out."

"What?" he asked, incredulous.

"There's something that Audrey wants you to know."

He glared at Audrey. "I really don't care what this bitch has to say."

"Just listen," Sydney said.

He sighed before he looked at Audrey. "What?"

She twisted her hands together. "I didn't cheat on you, Coen. I swear."

He rolled his eyes. "We already talked about this a million times."

"And I wasn't lying. Please believe me."

He looked away from her.

Sydney grabbed his hand. "I believe her."

"You do?" he asked.

She nodded. "It all makes sense. She was trying so hard to get you back because you broke up over a rumor, not a fact. I think she's telling the truth."

"Fine. I believe you," he said.

Audrey looked at him. "Please give me another chance, Coen."

"I'm engaged," he said quickly. "I'm getting married."

"The truth changes nothing?" she asked sadly. "That isn't fair."

He ran his fingers through his hair. "I'm sorry, Audrey. Everything is different now. I don't feel the same anymore. I'm totally in love with Sydney. She's the only woman that I want for the rest of my life. And even if I did still have feelings for you, I wouldn't be with you. You harassed Sydney, poured syrup in her hair like a teenager, and demolished her car. How could I ever be with someone as horrible as that? Sydney refused to hit you or rat you out, being the better person. When I wanted to yell at you, she wouldn't let me. It's obvious who the better choice is."

"That's enough," Sydney whispered.

Audrey started to cry again. "I'm sorry about everything."

He was quiet for a long time. "It's okay. I forgive you. But that's all I can offer you. Sydney has my heart, for now and for always."

Audrey clutched her stomach and looked at the floor, shaking.

"Hug her," Sydney whispered.

"Fuck no," he snapped.

"Just do it," she said as she nudged him.

He glared at her. "I'm only doing this because you told me to."

"I know. Go."

He sighed then approached her, wrapping his arms around her. She cried into his shoulder while Henry and Sydney stepped back, giving them some privacy. After a long time, she finally pulled away from him.

"I really am sorry, Coen."

"I know," he said as he dropped his hands.

"Can we be friends?"

He shook his head. "I'm sorry. I forgive you for what you did, but I don't want any type of relationship with you. I wish you well and hope you find happiness."

She nodded. "Okay."

"Goodbye, Audrey."

"Yeah," she said as she turned away.

Coen came back to Sydney and wiped his hands on his jeans, like he just picked up fresh manure. "I'm so glad that's over."

"Me too," Henry said.

Coen stared at her for a long time. "You're a much bigger person than I could ever imagine."

"Everyone is good. They just do evil things sometimes."

"That's one opinion," Henry said sarcastically.

Coen wrapped his arms around her waist. "I'm sorry that you had to deal with all of that. Thank you for putting up with it."

"I would do anything for you."

"I know you would." He kissed her forehead. "Let's get to class."

9

Sydney packed all her essentials for the trip out to sea. She still couldn't believe that the brilliant Dr. Goldstein actually invited her to accompany him on the trip. She packed layers because she didn't know how cold it would get out there. She also brought her snorkeling and swimming gear just in case she was allowed to take a dip in the ocean.

Coen watched her pack. "Three days sounds horrible."

"It's going to be so awesome," she said as she shoved her jacket inside the bag.

"I can't go three days without having sex."

"You have your hand, don't you?"

"It's not the same thing at all."

"You'll be okay. I won't be gone for long." She grabbed the bag and carried it to his car. When she opened the back, she saw a bunch of luggage inside. "Babe, what's this for?"

"Oh. I forgot to mention that I'm going."

Her eyes lit up. "You are?"

"Of course."

"How did that happen?"

"I asked Dr. Goldstein if I could go."

"And he just said yes?"

"Yep."

"Wow. You should have been a car salesman. You know how to persuade people."

He laughed. "I don't know about that." He threw her other belongings inside.

"I'm so happy you're coming. It's going to be so amazing."

"You are?"

"So happy. Now we don't have to wait for three days."

He raised an eyebrow. "That's gonna be hard to pull off."

"Well, people have to sleep sometime."

He smiled. "I like it. We'll have to sneak around."

She pushed her bag all the way to the back seat. Her ring caught her attention as it reflected the light. He hadn't asked for it back and she hadn't offered to return it to him. The issue with Audrey was settled. There was really no reason to keep up the charade. Even if she learned the truth, Sydney knew she wouldn't lash out at their relationship again. But a part of her didn't want to give it back. She felt like a psycho, clingy girlfriend, but she couldn't do it. She hadn't removed it from her finger. She would wait until Coen asked for it back. Until then, she would act like she just forgot. She wasn't sure what she was hoping for. There's no way he was ready to get married. They had only been together for a few months. And after she told him the news of her family's visit, she wasn't sure if he would even want to marry her. They were set to arrive a few days before Thanksgiving and she still hadn't mentioned it to him. She knew how pissed he was going to be. "We should get going."

"Okay," he said as he walked to the passenger door and opened it for her. After she was settled, he walked back to his side then drove toward the loading dock that was connected to the aquarium near the wharf.

When they got out, Coen carried most of the luggage until they reached the medium sized boat. It was almost as big as a yacht, but a little smaller. There were two levels, along with another boat attached to it. Sydney felt the excitement flood through her as Dr. Goldstein walked down the ramp.

"Hello, Dr. Goldstein," she said as she shook his hand. "Thank you so much for allowing me to attend this trip. It means so much to me. I won't let you down."

He smiled at her then pulled his hand away. "I'm excited to have you, Sydney. Thank you for your interest." He turned to Coen. "Hey."

"Hey."

"You packed your whole life?"

"Most of them are Sydney's," he explained.

"Sure," he said sarcastically.

Sydney raised an eyebrow. They were particularly chummy for hardly knowing each other.

"My hedges are getting tall," Dr. Goldstein said to Coen as he tapped him on the shoulder.

"The month is already over."

"Next time, I'll make it two," he said with a smile.

Coen carried their bags up the ramp and down to the deck below. He put their belongings on the two bunk beds.

"What was that?" she asked.

"What do you mean?" he asked, avoiding her gaze.

"Do you know Dr. Goldstein?"

He sat on the bed and felt the springs. "They are quiet. Good."

Coen would never lie to her, so his attempt at avoiding the question altogether was evidence of his secrecy.

"I asked you a question, Coen."

He was quiet for a moment. "Yes, I know him."

"How?"

He sighed and ran his fingers through his hair. "Don't ask me that."

"I just did."

He looked up at her with a saddened expression. "I don't want you to know."

"Too bad."

"Damn," he said as he stood up. "He's my uncle."

"Dr. Goldstein is your uncle?" she asked, amazed.

"Yeah."

"Why didn't you tell me before?"

He shrugged. "It just didn't come up."

Her mind started to race. Why would he want to hide that from her? It definitely wasn't embarrassing. If anything, his relation to him would have only impressed her. Then it hit her. "You asked him to take me."

"That's why I didn't want to tell you."

She hugged him and he flinched, surprised at her affection. "Thank you. That was so sweet, Coen."

He breathed a sigh of relief. "I thought you would be mad at me."

"Not at all. That means so much to me. I would have scrubbed toilets for a whole month just to get a spot here."

He kissed her forehead. "I'm just glad you aren't mad."

"No. Thank you so much. And I'll show him my talents when we work together. He'll be glad that he brought me along."

He smiled. "That's my girl."

She stared at him for a long time, moved by his obvious love for her. Dr. Goldstein invited her months ago. Even then, he was willing to do anything for her. She ran her hands up his chest. "I wish we were alone right now."

He raised an eyebrow. "If I knew this was the response I was going to get, I would have told you a long time ago."

"I'll show you my appreciation when we get home."

"Ooh. This is getting even better." He kissed her on the forehead. "I'll be right back. Organize our stuff."

"Okay," she said. After he was gone, she organized her belongings and took out her waterproof folders and notebooks, not wanting them to get destroyed from the waves that crashed over the rail. She was so excited that her hands were shaking. She always wanted to be a researcher and hoped she would get enough grant money to have her own expeditions. She wanted to study the fish in the Great Barrier Reef on the coast of Australia but she probably wouldn't be able to afford it for many years.

Coen returned a moment later. "I have wonderful news."

"What?"

The other two crew members on the boat are married so they're sharing their own quarters. My uncle obviously has the captain's room."

"So?"

He grabbed her bag from the top bed then pulled it to the bottom one. "We're going to be alone every night."

"Isn't that weird because of your uncle?"

"I don't care what he thinks, and he doesn't care what I do. I'm a guy in college. Of course I'm going to have sex with my girlfriend. Even if people were in here, I would have done it anyway."

"You're so classy," she said sarcastically.

"I'm just always hot for you. And don't act like you would have survived three days without getting some. You are worse than I am."

"You have a point."

"So, the ship is about to leave. Let's go to the portside."

"Okay," she said as she followed him.

Coen's uncle drove the boat out to sea, far enough away that the waves became choppy and there were no other boats around them. Sydney marked down the coordinates for future reference. The air became saltier as they moved away from the shore but Sydney enjoyed the scent.

When Dr. Goldstein was on deck, she basically followed him like a stalker, assisting him in any way she could. Whenever he opened a textbook and browsed through it, she scribbled quick notes about what he was reading. When she found his research notebook, she practically memorized every word. Coen watched her with a smirk on his face, happy that he made this happen for her. She ignored him completely, but in light of her joy, he didn't care.

When Dr. Goldstein took zero readings, Sydney organized all the data into a spreadsheet and sterilized the equipment before she put it away. Every time he took a step forward, Sydney was already there, beating him to the punch. Her obsession was slightly embarrassing but Coen didn't tease her about it. She obviously loved this.

When their day was completed, they ate processed food stored in the cabinets and a small vegetarian stew. Sydney was relieved that everyone besides Coen didn't eat meat. If there wasn't any food to accommodate her, she would have had to starve or just eat it anyway. After they marked anchor, everyone retired to bed. When Coen moved to the stairway, he realized she wasn't following him. She sat on the deck and looked across the ocean, the breeze running through her hair.

"Ready for bed?" he asked as he sat beside her.

"How can I sleep when I know this is out here?"

The waves were docile and rocked the boat slightly, not enough to be distracting. Even though it was pitch black, it was still beautiful. The wide expanse of the ocean never seemed to end. The greatest part of the moment was the stars. There were so many, shining brighter than the sun itself.

When he looked at her, he saw the moonlight fall on her face, highlighting her features and strained cheekbones. Her brown hair cascaded around her, making her look hypnotic and awe inspiriting. Coen had seen many beautiful women in his life, but she was definitely the fairest of them all.

"It's beautiful," he whispered.

"I'll never forget this moment."

"Nor will I." He lay down on the deck, facing the heavens. She settled beside him and rested her hands on her stomach.

"There are so many," she whispered, looking at the stars.

"I couldn't count them."

"I can't believe it."

He grabbed her left hand and held it within his own. His fingers caressed the ring on her finger, feeling the band. Her heart raced when she felt him. She didn't want him to ask for his ring back but she suspected he would. His uncle hadn't commented on the ring, which she thought was odd. It was hard to miss.

He leaned over her. "You know what I want to do?"

She smiled. "I can guess."

"This is such a beautiful place and I want to do something beautiful with you."

"What if someone comes?"

"I couldn't care less." He pulled down her shorts and underwear then removed his own. They both kept their shirts on, just in case. His left hand grabbed hers, his fingers resting against the ring, then he inserted himself inside of her.

She wanted to gasp but she didn't. She kept it lodged in her throat so she wouldn't make a sound.

He pressed his forehead against hers, rocking into her in sync with the waves of the boat. Her body felt warm against his, perfect. He had never felt a deeper connection to someone. She was beautiful, amazing, perfect, the list went on. He never expected to find someone he loved unconditionally so early in his life.

The light of the stars fell on her face and reflected in her eyes, making them look wilder and more vibrant than ever before. His gaze locked onto hers and he saw his entire future within her depths. He wanted to do this every night for the rest of his life. There was no one else for him. Even though he sometimes felt jealous knowing that Henry was equally obsessed with her, he couldn't blame him for falling in love with Sydney. She was too wonderful and magnificent to ignore. When he felt his orgasm start, he held it back, waiting for her to go first.

Having sex in absolute silence was more arousing than listening to her scream his name. He could hear every breath that escaped her lips, every slight moan that burst from her throat, and he heard the sound of his cock moving inside her, the moisture sliding in and out.

When she closed her mouth overs his, he knew she was trying to be quiet. He felt her hot breaths increase as she crumbled underneath him, feeling her body dissolve under his movement. Her fingers dug into her skin, her hips moved harder as she enjoyed the explosion that radiated through her body. When she was done, she relaxed her hold, and Coen let himself go, staring into her beautiful green eyes the entire time.

They stared at each other as they caught their breath, unable to break the connection that they both felt. When he was inside her, he felt like he was a part of her, that she ended and he began. Her soul touched his, massaging his heart as he made love to her, declaring his undying love for her. He didn't know what was more beautiful. The majestic glory of their location in the middle of the ocean, or the pure and wonderful act they just committed.

10

The next morning, Coen woke up to Sydney sprawled in his arms. Her naked skin touched his and he felt warm and lazy. He wished they were back at her house, lying there all day until the sun went down again.

She fell asleep while they lay on the deck, so he carried her to their quarters down below. When he undressed her, she didn't wake up because she was so exhausted. Running around, chasing Dr. Goldstein everywhere really took it out of her.

When she woke up, she kissed him then yawned.

"Sleep well?"

"I always sleep well when I'm in your arms."

"I'm glad."

She rose from the bed then dressed herself in her gear. "We are going to see a great white shark today."

"Are you scared?"

"No."

"I would be."

"I'm not going to swim with it while we're feeding it."

"Or swim with it period."

"Why not?"

He raised an eyebrow. "Because it could eat you."

"It won't eat me."

"And how do you know that?"

"Because I'm not a seal."

"When a shark is hungry, it's not gonna care what you are."

"You are overreacting."

"Okay. Now I know you aren't joking."

"What?"

"I admire your bravery and courage, but this is suicide. Don't jump in the water, especially after bait has been thrown in."

"I'm not stupid."

"Then why are you even considering it?"

"It's my greatest dream to swim with a shark."

"Go inside a cage."

"It's not the same."

"Well, it's the best you are going to get."

She stared at him. "If you think you can tell me what to do, then you have another thing coming."

"I don't tell you what do, but this is an exception. You aren't swimming with a fucking shark."

"You don't boss me around."

"I'm not! I'm trying to talk some sense into you."

"You won't change my mind."

"Yes, I will."

"No."

"I love you. Please don't hurt me."

"Don't pull the 'hurt' card."

"Well, I'm gonna. If you jump in that water, I'll just have to jump in after you."

"That makes no sense."

"If you die, I die too."

"Now you're being crazy."

"I'll do it if I have to."

"I understand the risks that I'm taking. I don't want you to put your life in danger unless it's something you believe in."

"I do believe in it. Where you go, I go."

She sighed. "Coen, knock it off."

"No. You can't tell me what to do."

"You're so annoying, you know that?"

"I love you. I can't live without you."

She shook her head then left their quarters, leaving him standing there.

After they had breakfast, they started work immediately. Dr. Goldstein caught a few smaller sharks then pulled them on deck. Sydney took measurements of their rectal glands and determined the salt concentration of some of the sharks. When the concentration was high, she would tag them then place them in a special filtered tank below deck until they returned home. They took a variety of samples until they examined a hundred different small sharks. When they felt the boat rock, Dr. Goldstein stood up and looked overboard.

"We got a big one."

Sydney jumped to her feet then looked over the rail. Unable to stop himself, Coen grabbed her arm and held her steady just in case he had to pull her out of the way. A sixteen foot shark swam around the boat, eating the leftover bait. His fin stuck out high from the water and carved the surface with its tip.

"It's so beautiful," Sydney said, mesmerized.

"Would you like to get a closer look?" Dr. Goldstein offered.

"Yes!" she screamed.

"Put on your wet suit and get your gear."

Coen felt his heart accelerate. She was going to be inside a cage but it still made him feel nervous. Anything could happen. With lightning speed, she changed and hooked all her scuba gear up. Coen double checked everything just to make sure it was working properly. They threw the cage over the side then dropped the bloody meat in the water. Immediately, the shark swam closer, chomping down on the grub.

Sydney went to the edge then placed her feet over the rail. Coen grabbed onto her until she slid inside the cage.

When Sydney was underwater, she took a deep breath from the mouth piece and watched the shark swim a few inches from the edge of the cage. His razor sharp teeth tore the fish to pieces. There were two rows of teeth, both equally sharp and frightening. When it opened its mouth to bite the cage, she saw the inside of its gills and the dark hole that reached deep inside him. He was so humungous that she couldn't even comprehend it. It left her speechless. The shark swam around the cage and she watched it, mesmerized. It was one of the most beautiful things she had ever seen. When the shark had its fill, it swam away and disappeared. It was such an amazing sight that she stayed rooted to the spot. After a moment, she regained her composure then swam to the top of the cage. Coen pulled her out and helped her to the deck.

"What was it like?"

"I can't even explain," she said breathlessly.

Dr. Goldstein smiled. "I like your passion. It's the backbone of research. You will make a great candidate someday."

Her eyes lit up like stars. Her day just kept getting better.

They spent the rest of the day gathering results then Sydney stayed up late to consolidate everything into spreadsheets. She lay beside Coen in bed while he snuggled next to her. He waited for her to finish so they could make love. Now he couldn't sleep unless he was satisfied.

"You almost done?" he asked.

"No. I want to finish before we go home tomorrow. I want to impress him so he'll invite me to his lab."

"Can we make love first?"

"I'm busy, Coen. It will have to wait until tomorrow."

He sighed. "I can't even imagine what would happen if I said that to you. You would just crawl on top of me anyway."

"Fine." She moved her computer then flipped onto her stomach, facing the screen. She continued to enter data in. "There. Go ahead."

"Well, this is romantic."

"Take it or leave it."

He stared at her ass for a moment before he moved on top of her. He wanted to wait until she was in the moment too but his twitching cock just wanted to get off. Coen rubbed her clitoris for a while until she was wet. Then, he slipped inside her while he moved into her, hard and fast like he wanted to. He wasn't worried about satisfying her because she seemed preoccupied anyway, so he just tried to get himself off.

When her hands stopped typing and she moaned, he knew she wanted to come.

"I change my mind," she whispered.

He fucked her harder. "I thought you would." He pressed his mouth against her ear and whispered words of love while he thrust into her.

When she gripped the back of his neck and moaned, he knew she was there. Her explosion made her shake and she moved her ass against him as she pulled out every ounce of pleasure she could. When her gasps disappeared, he exploded inside of her, filling her completely. She gasped again, loving it when he released inside her. He pulled out then wiped himself off before he lay down and closed his eyes.

"Good night," he said.

She fixed her hair. "Night."

He kissed her shoulder. "I love you, seahorse."

"I love you too."

Coen fell asleep, lulled into unconsciousness by the rocking of the waves.

11

When they returned to the shore, Sydney thanked Dr. Goldstein for letting her come along. She was so grateful to experience so much research in such a short amount of time. Coen knew his uncle had become fond of Sydney as soon as she stepped on that boat even though he would never admit it.

"I would love it if you would be my lab assistant."

"Are you serious?" she blurted.

He laughed. "I'll let them know at work tomorrow. You can hang up those ugly overalls that you have to wear."

"Thank you so much," she said as she shook his hand vigorously.

Dr. Goldstein looked at Coen. "Keep this one around."

Coen nodded. "I will."

He walked off the ramp and headed to the parking lot. Coen grabbed their belongings and shoved it all into the back of the truck. Sydney rambled on about every aspect of the trip and her new job at the aquarium. He heard everything before, but he humored her by listening again. She was already so excited and he didn't want to ruin that for her.

When they got home, she was still chattering about it as Coen carried all her bags inside. Normally she helped, but she was too happy about her new position to really think about it. Coen didn't mind. He didn't like it when she carried anything anyway.

Sydney walked into her room then picked up her cell phone. She left it behind because she didn't want it to get wet, and besides, there was no reception out there. When she checked her voicemails, she had a message from her mother, saying they would be coming for Thanksgiving. She sighed when she listened to it. Her wonderful day was ruined as she listened to the sound of her mother's voice. She wasn't even her mother. She was by blood, but not by any other aspect. Depressed, she put the phone down and stared at the wall.

"Wow. Talk about a mood swing," Coen said as he grabbed the laundry basket and threw her dirty stuff inside.

"I'm sorry."

"What's gotten you so down?"

"Nothing."

He clenched his fists. "You know I hate being lied to. Stop the bullshit."

"Well, I don't want to talk about it so don't ask."

He sighed. "I thought we were past this. I thought you told me everything. What else are you hiding from me?" He sat beside her and grabbed her hand. "We tell each other everything."

She looked away. "It's going to make you mad."

"I don't like the sound of that."

"Neither do I."

"What if I promise not to get mad?"

"I can't make you do that—not this time."

"Now you have to tell me."

She rubbed her fingers together and admired the ring on her finger. If he never asked her to take it off, then she was never going to. It fit her perfectly, just the right size. She was glad she wore it in the ocean, letting it touch something as beautiful as itself, an element different than its own.

"Syd?"

"My mom and stepdad are coming for Thanksgiving."

He said nothing for a long time. He stared at her, his eyes wide with impending ferocity. She didn't look at him, but felt that hateful stare burn a hole through her skin. He jumped up. "Why the fuck are they coming here?"

"They wanted to."

"And you couldn't just say no."

"I did but my stepdad got mad."

"And why the hell should you care?"

"Because he'll hurt my mom."

He grabbed his hair and almost yanked the strands out of his skull. "You've got to be kidding me. That bitch stood aside and let you be beaten countless times. Why should she get any of your sympathy? She's in that relationship because she chooses to be. You shouldn't give a shit about her."

"I can't let that happen."

Coen punched his fist against the wall. It made a loud thud. When pulled it away, there was blood on the wall. "Call them and tell them they aren't coming."

"It's too late now."

He paced around the room, his eyes wide. "I can't believe this is happening."

"I'm sorry."

He ignored her.

"Please stop. You're scaring me."

"Too bad," he snapped.

She hugged a pillow to her chest then stared at the floor.

"I'm staying here the entire time they're here."

"What?" she said as she looked at him.

"You can't argue with me. I sleep here, facing the door. You do not leave my presence until they are on that plane and back to hell."

"We aren't married."

"Your point?"

"My stepfather would never allow that."

He glared at her. "Sydney, you are an adult that takes care of herself. You don't need them for anything. If they don't like it, they can go somewhere else."

"Then he might hit me."

"Then you hit back, Syd. You beat the shit out of him. That's if you can get to him before me." His eyes had a maniacal gleam to them.

"I can't ask you to put up with this, Coen."

"We are a team. I won't let them hurt you."

"You can't hurt them either."

"I promise that I won't attack them. I'm allowed to retaliate."

"You don't deserve this."

He kneeled before her. "I love you no matter what. I don't care where you come from or about your past. I'm in love with you, not anything else. I will put up with all this bullshit just so I get to keep you."

She took a deep breath. "What about your family?"

"Well, I wanted you to come over for Thanksgiving, but I guess that won't be happening."

"But I can't take you away from them. I'm already hogging you."

"They'll understand, Sydney."

"Please don't tell them the truth," she begged.

"How else am I supposed to explain my absence?"

"Please don't. I don't want them to hate me or think I'm not good enough for you."

"They would never think that. They know I love you for the strong woman you've become, not the weak girl you used to be. They would never hold your past against you. Believe me."

"I don't know."

"I won't tell them if you don't want me to, but I promise they won't judge you if they know the truth. Plus, it will make my life easier."

She sighed. "Okay."

He kissed her. "It's going to be okay, Syd. They'll be gone in a few days and I'll be beside you the entire time."

"I don't know what I would do without you."

"You'll never have to find out."

12

As the days trickled by and Thanksgiving approached, Sydney became more stressed. Her new job didn't distract her, and neither did Coen or her friends. Flashbacks of her childhood came flooding back to her during the most random times. When Henry was talking to her, memories of her stepfather throwing a bottle of beer at her splashed across her eyes. When he asked what was bothering her, she always said it was nothing.

Coen noticed her pain but didn't address the subject. There was nothing he could say to make her feel better about the ordeal. He wasn't even sure how he felt about it. He wanted to kill all three of them and blame it on a horrific accident of some sort.

Their lovemaking wasn't as intense and powerful as it normally was. In fact, she was dry. He could hardly get her in the mood. Most of the time, she just had a stoic expression on her face, like she was thinking of something else. Coen tried not to let it bother him but it did. That connection with her always calmed him and made him feel at peace with the world. He jacked off, thinking about her, but it was never the same. He could barely come doing that because he missed the real thing so much. But he wouldn't pressure Sydney into doing something she wasn't comfortable with.

At lunchtime on the last day of school, Coen was sitting next to her but he didn't look at her or speak to her. Henry picked up on the tension between them.

"Is everything okay?" he asked.

Sydney stared at the table like she hadn't heard him.

"Yeah. We're fine," Coen answered.

Henry ignored him, his eyes set on Sydney. "Syd?"

She looked up. "What's up?"

"Did you hear me?"

"Uh—no."

"I know something's wrong. Is there anything I can do?"

She smiled at him, but it was very weak. "No, Henry."

"Are you and Coen having problems?"

"No. We are just as in love as we've always been."

Nancy raised an eyebrow. "Doesn't seem like it."

"I'm just—not in the mood," she answered.

They fell silent. Coen ran his hand up and down her arm, trying to wake her up from this dead stupor.

"How was the research?" Henry asked. "You still haven't told us about it."

She sighed. "It was fine."

"Fine?" he asked.

Coen shook his head, silently begging her two friends just to drop it.

Henry sighed then did just that.

Sydney stared out the window, thinking about the pain that was about to come. She finally blocked out her past because of Coen, but now it returned with a vengeance. It seemed like she would never be free of them. She wasn't going to put up with this anymore. As soon as she thought about seeing them again, she returned to her role as the weak victim, talking only when spoken to, and curling up in a ball in a defensive way. She refused to do that again. This time, if she was hit, she would hit back. If

119

her mother still didn't show remorse or care about what happened to Sydney, then she could go fuck herself too. Coen was right. He was her family now—not them.

When classes were finally over for the day, everyone talked about going home to see their families, whether it was on the mainland or internationally. Sydney wished she was going to Coen's house to have Thanksgiving with his family. She hadn't met them yet but she knew she would love them. Anyone was wonderful compared to her own family.

She walked to the parking lot and saw all her friends gathered around.

"Hey," Henry said with a smile. "The day is finally over! We get a four day weekend."

"Yeah," she said sadly.

"What are you doing for turkey day?" he asked.

"Well, my family is coming over."

"From the mainland?"

"Yeah."

"Oh, cool."

She nodded.

He saw the despair in her eyes. "Is that why you've been sad for the past few days?"

Henry knew her just as well as Coen did. "Yeah."

"Do you want to talk about it?"

"No. Coen will take care of me."

"Okay. You are always welcome with me and my family if you want to spend Thanksgiving with us."

She smiled. "Thank you, Henry. But I'll be okay."

He wrapped his arms around her and hugged her. It had been so long since they touched each other that it felt different. His touch actually felt friendly, not lustful. She laid her head on his chest and closed her eyes. If she just focused on all the beautiful things she found in her life, she would be okay. She made a life for herself on her own. The evil and horrific things that happened to her shouldn't destroy her.

"I love you," she whispered.

He rested his head on hers. "I love you too."

Coen was nearby but he didn't interfere with their moment. The affection didn't bother him either. Henry wouldn't try to steal her away, and even if he tried, he would be unsuccessful because Sydney only loved him.

"I'll save you some of my mom's apple pie," he said into her ear.

"I love her pies."

"She said she'll make one just for you this year."

"She did?"

"I'll send it over as soon as the holiday is over."

"I'm going to get fat."

"I'm sure Coen will enjoy it anyway."

She smiled then pulled away.

Coen came over and wrapped his arm around her waist. "Ready to go home, baby?"

"Yeah," she said quietly. She hugged Nancy and Laura before they drove home to the shack on the dirt road.

"Where are they going to stay?" he asked.

"In the living room or the entryway."

"You aren't giving them your bedroom, right?"

"No," she said firmly.

"Good."

121

They went to the store and bought all the groceries they needed to cook Thanksgiving dinner. They prepped most of it so they wouldn't have to worry about it on Thanksgiving . Coen helped make the turkey and the stuffing. When everything was finished, they were both tired.

Sydney took off her apron. "Thank you for helping me."

"You don't need to thank me, seahorse."

They moved to the couch then lay under a blanket, watching television. She curled up next to him and thought about all the training she went through. She never actually expected to use it. It just made her feel better, helped her sleep at night, but now she might need to.

When it became late, Coen picked her up and carried her into her bedroom, tucking her in before he lay down beside her.

The movement woke her up. "I'm not scared."

He stared at her. "You shouldn't be."

"And not because you're going to be there."

"I know. You got this, Sydney."

"I do."

13

In the middle of the night, Sydney opened her eyes and stared at the ceiling. Long shadows stretched across the walls, making them look like stretching hands. She glanced at Coen, sleeping peacefully beside her. His chest rose and fell with the steady cadence of his lungs. In sleep, his mouth was relaxed and his lips were pressed together in a tight line. The grooves of his lips reminded her of the desert landscape, the trail of a slithering snake. Ever since they started dating, his lips started to dry and crack from their excessive kissing. Eventually, he got his own ChapStick and had it in the pocket of his jeans.

She crawled out of bed without disturbing him. The blankets were ruffled around his waist, exposing his hard chest. She kissed the skin over his heart before she dressed herself and left out the front door, closing it quietly behind her.

The waves pounded against the shore as the moon shined overhead. It was a beacon of light, showing her the mounds in the sand and the bramble from nearby trees. She sat on the beach and tucked her toes under the sand, feeling the grains lodge in the crevasses of her feet. She always had sand everywhere, her hair, her eyelashes, and underneath her nails. Now the dirt didn't bother her. When she was clean, she felt awkward.

Coen always made her feel safe and sound, but he couldn't solve all her problems. She knew he would take a bullet to the chest, a knife in the back just to spare her any pain, but she needed to deal with this on her own. This was her issue and it needed to be resolved.

Sydney was always willing to grant forgiveness to anyone, whether they asked for it or not, but she didn't think that was possible in regards to her family. When she remembered everything she suffered through, her heart hardened. Everything came back to her in a flash, blinding her eyes and dominating her mind.

"Why are you late?" Dan asked.

She stopped on the doorstep, tightening her hold on her backpack. She tried out for the swim team just so she could be at school longer. She didn't like being wet, but it was the better alternative. "I'm on the swim team. I already said that."

He squeezed the empty beer can then tossed it on the floor. It was only five in the afternoon, but he was already drunk. "And I forbade you from doing that."

She said nothing. They didn't have to pick her up or drop her off. And when she was home, they ignored her anyway. There was no reason why she couldn't play sports. "But I like it," she whispered.

He glared at her, his shoulders tensing. "Your father said no."

She stepped back. Every time he said this, her response was always the same. She knew she should bite her tongue but she couldn't. She believed in it too much to let it go. "You're not my father."

"What did you say?" He held up his hand, threatening to slap her across the face.

Her mother emerged from the kitchen, drying a plate in her hands. "What's going on?"

"Your daughter is being a bitch—like usual," he said, his eyes still glued to Sydney's. "Now what did you say?"

Sydney glanced at her mother, silently asking for help. When she said nothing, her face completely stoic, Sydney knew she was on her own.

"I asked you a question!" he said, his hand still raised.

She took a deep breath, preparing for the collision against her face. It would turn the skin red, burning like hot wax. Her stepfather never did any extensive damage to her face, like giving her black eyes to get him in trouble. During the summer vacation, he wasn't so selective. She kept her gaze to the floor. "You aren't my father."

His hand collided against her face with enough force to push her to the ground. She placed her hand over her cheek as she gasped, feeling the tears sting her eyes. He ripped her hand from her face then slapped her again. She yelped, unable to ignore the pain, and lay on the floor, absolutely still. Her mother walked back into the kitchen, not reacting in any way.

Dan grabbed her wrist and yanked her to her feet. He pressed his face against hers. "I will slap you as many times as it takes." He pushed her back, making her stumble down the hallway. She got to her feet and bolted to her room, closing it behind her. Her tears blurred her vision as they fell, burning her eyes. She sat at the edge of her bed and stared at the mirror of her closet. Her face became even redder with obvious despair. She was miserable there, unable to escape. Instead of eating dinner with her family, she decided to hide in her room. She would rather starve than sit at the table with the people she hated most.

"Dinner's ready," her mom said as she knocked on the door.

"I'm not hungry."

"Come on."

"No."

"Do you want me to tell Dan that?" Her threat hung in the air.

She wiped her tears away. "I'm coming."

"Good girl."

She clenched her fists before leaving her room. She hated being treated like a dog. She walked into the hallway and sat at the dinner table. Johnny, her infuriating stepbrother, sat next to her. Dan never yelled at his own son, treating him like a cherished child. Even her mom was sweet to him.

His hand moved under the table and rested on Sydney's thigh. She pushed it away then crossed her legs. His hand returned with a gentle squeeze. She eyed the knife on the table, considering whether she should pick it up and stab him through the eye, but resisted her bloodlust.

"How was school?" her mother asked.

"Good," Johnny said, inching his hand closer to the apex of her thighs.

Sydney said nothing. Neither of them cared anyway. She didn't understand why they didn't just kill her. They obviously hated her. She would prefer to be buried six feet under than live in that hell.

Sydney picked at her food, but didn't eat anything. She was too depressed to have an appetite. She was thin and sickly but didn't have a choice. She wasn't given a sack lunch or money to buy food in the cafeteria. And when she looked at the disgusting look on her stepfather's face, her stomach hurt too much to eat a single bite.

"Eat," he said before he drank from his beer.

She knew his command was for her. Everyone else was eating. Obediently, she shoved the food into her mouth.

"Good girl."

She clenched her jaw.

Johnny's hand moved further up her leg.

She inhaled her food then stood up from the table, about to retreat to her room.

"You aren't dismissed."

"Fuck you," she snapped.

He stood up, his arms shaking. "How dare you say that to your father!"

"Go to hell," she said without turning around.

Dan chased after her while Johnny grinned from ear to ear. Her mother didn't stop eating her dinner, acting like the entire situation was normal. He grabbed the bat leaning against the refrigerator. She heard him swing it in his arms as he chased her. She sprinted to her room then shut the door behind her, her hands shaking and her heart accelerating. She moved her dresser in front of the door but she knew he would break through. The lock on her bedroom had been disabled years ago.

He shoved his entire body into the door until the dressed tipped over, sending everything on top to the wooden ground. Her jewelry, pictures, hair bands, and pencils rolled onto the floor. Glass was shattered. The door was pushed open and he finally made it inside. He spun the bat around his wrist while he stared her down.

She moved against the wall and slid to the floor, knowing there was nowhere she could run or hide. He would beat her like he always did, and she would cry to herself, knowing she deserved the pain. She was responsible for her father's death so she deserved to be beaten. If she hadn't run away, none of this would be happening. It was that moment when her spirit broke. Never again would she defy him or stand up for what she believed in. If she did, he would kill her.

When the memory left her mind, the sight of the ocean waves caught her attention. They rose up the beach and started to inch closer to her toes, the tide increasing. The wind still ruffled her hair. There was no way to determine how much time had passed. Her memory seemed to last for a short minute, but the moon in the sky had moved, veering farther to the left.

She wrapped her arms around herself because she felt cold, frozen. Her greatest enemies were returning to her. This time, they were coming into the shack that she had made into a home. Her most beautiful moments of life were made on this beach and in that house. She had friends who loved her, a boyfriend who would die for her. It was almost a desecration to the holy land to let them even step on the grounds.

The past wouldn't repeat itself in this new life. If her stepfather made a move against her, she would retaliate, verbally and physically. Everything was different. She was different. For the first time, she wanted him to hit her. She smiled in the darkness, only the ocean acting as her witness. The storm had come but she would was breaking through the waves. She looked forward to tomorrow. It couldn't come soon enough.

14

When the knock sounded on the door, Sydney flinched in her seat on the couch. Coen stood up and they both walked to the door. Before they reached for the handle, Coen grabbed her shoulders and turned her body to face him.

"They can't hurt you, Syd."

"I know."

He pressed his forehead against hers. "I'll be here the entire time. Please don't be scared."

She grabbed her engagement ring to pull it off. "I should return this so they don't get the wrong impression."

He steadied her hand. "Keep it. Tell them we are engaged and we live together. That will explain why I'm here all the time."

She left the ring on her finger. "Are you sure?"

"Yeah." He rubbed his nose against hers. "Absolutely."

"Okay." She took a deep breath and turned toward the door. When she placed her hand on the handle, it stayed there for a long time, not moving. After her resolve flooded through her body, she found the strength to turn it.

Her mother's face was the first thing she saw. She had the same sandy-brown hair that Sydney had and even the same forest green eyes. Her body wasn't what it used to be. She had gained significant weight, making her at least eighty pounds heavier. Since she was so short, it made her look rounder. She smiled at her daughter. Her teeth were stained yellow from liquor and cigarettes.

"Happy Thanksgiving," her mother said as she extended her arms, wrapping them around Sydney.

Sydney stood there awkwardly for a moment, unsure how to respond. She couldn't remember the last time she embraced her mother. She wasn't expecting the affection but gave her a hug anyway. "Happy Thanksgiving."

Her mother pulled away. "Still plump like usual."

Sydney opened her mouth to speak, but Coen spoke first. "And absolutely gorgeous," he said, hooking his arm around her waist.

Her mother looked at him. "And who is this?"

Sydney smiled at him then looked at her mother. "My boy—fiancé."

Her mother raised an eyebrow. "You're engaged?"

"Yeah," Sydney said with a smile. It was all an act but the idea made her happy anyway.

Coen extended his hand. "I'm Coen. It's nice to meet you, Mrs. Morris."

"Call me Denise," she said quickly.

He nodded. "Denise it is."

She stared at him for a long time, practically gawking at him. "And you want to marry my daughter?" The disbelief in her voice was evident. Sydney knew she shouldn't let it bother her but it did. She always felt like she wasn't good enough for Coen, that he was too good-looking for her. His inner beauty triumphed over hers as well. She never met someone so selfless and loyal.

Coen's hand gripped her side but his voice didn't betray his annoyance. "I can't believe it either. I wasn't

131

sure why she picked me of all people. She could have whoever she wanted."

Her mother nodded, but said nothing. She stepped aside and let Johnny enter the room. He smiled at Sydney and his eyes trailed across her body, taking in her curves, especially the roundness of her breasts. When he used to harass her, he was always obsessed with her tits. They were even bigger since the last time he saw her. Sydney felt the lust boil from his skin as he gawked at her. He was bigger and taller than she remembered him. He was a year older than her and he never let that fact leave her knowledge.

"Hey," he said with a smile.

Coen extended his hand, a look of murder on his face. "Sydney's fiancé." He didn't say his name, just his title. Johnny's eyes flashed surprise for just a moment but then it disappeared, hiding under the surface. He didn't shake Coen's hand for a long time. Even though Coen promised he wouldn't be angry at her family or hit them, she was surprised he kept his word. After watching the tension in Coen's shoulders, she knew this was difficult for him, shaking the hand of his girlfriend's tormentor.

Johnny finally reached out and shook it, meeting Coen's gaze. His blond hair was short and spiked, revealing his blue eyes. There was vile and poison inside of him. He was psychotic. Just by looking at him, Sydney knew how twisted and evil he was. She hoped he had changed in two years, growing into a man that was trusted and respected. Obviously, she had been wrong. He still saw her as beneath him, someone he could take advantage of. When he saw her cry, he just smiled wider, even laughed. Sydney felt the emotions return to her but she forced them back to the pit of her stomach, hidden from everyone in the room.

When Coen pulled his hand away, he nodded to Johnny but there was no kindness in his look. His lips were pressed tightly together, like he wanted to stop himself from screaming every possibly profanity at him. Sydney knew Coen would kill him if he could get away with it. A part of her wished that was possible, that Johnny would die and be buried in a ditch somewhere, never to be seen again.

Johnny carried his bags into the house then deposited them on the floor. Sydney took a deep breath when she waited for the third member of her family to walk inside. She wasn't sure who she hated more, him or her stepbrother. It was a tie.

"Howdy," Dan said as he walked through the door, a large bag over one shoulder and another in the other hand. He stopped in front of Sydney and looked down at her. He didn't reach to embrace her and neither did she. The only time their skin touched was when he was slapping her across the face. Even in the spirit of the holiday, she couldn't force herself to be kind to him. All she could manage to do was speak.

"Happy Thanksgiving."

"Yeah," he said as he looked around the house. "Wow. This place is small."

"I said that many times," she said.

"But the beach is just a few feet away," her mother said.

It was obvious they only came to get a cheap vacation. They didn't care about seeing her or spending the holiday with her. Coen was right. She should have held her ground and just said no to begin with.

Coen waited for Dan to acknowledge him, but he kept examining the house, disappointment on his face. "I'm Coen," he said as he outstretched his hand.

Dan took it. He shook it without looking at him. He wore a long sleeve blue shirt and dark jeans. His heavy boots left a trial of filth on the floor. Sydney was normally picky about keeping her house clean, but it would be pointless to ask him to remove his shoes. It would just lead to an argument, one that she would lose.

"Dan," he said. He tossed the bags on the floor then walked further into the house.

Sydney sighed then followed them.

"When's dinner gonna be ready?" Johnny said as he sat on the couch and grabbed the remote, turning on a reality show.

"In a few minutes," Sydney answered tersely. She walked into the kitchen with Coen trailing behind her. Her family was so embarrassing that she wanted to cry. Her mom lit a cigarette and started to smoke it in the living room, and Dan placed his feet on the couch. Coen wouldn't want to be with her after these next few days were over. She would judge him if he stayed.

She pulled the turkey out of the oven and started to set the table. Coen helped her and moved all of the heavy stuff for her. He set the table and lit a few candles, trying to tone down the tension in the room as much as possible. Sydney was not looking forward to eating. It would be quiet time where they were facing each other at the table, forced to speak to one another. She made sure she had the turkey carver next to her wine glass.

Coen glanced at her, a slight smile on his face. Humiliated by everything that was happening, she looked away and tried not to cry. She opened the refrigerator and looked for something she didn't need. Wordlessly, he placed his hand on her back and kissed her neck, dissipating her tears. He placed his chest against her back and started to breathe, making her copy him. In a few seconds, she felt better. Coen grabbed her hand and pulled her away from the refrigerator, closing it.

"Dinner's ready," Coen said. Sydney was thankful for the announcement. Her throat was too dry to speak.

Dan clapped his hands together. "Bout' time."

Johnny walked to the table then dropped in his seat, scooping food onto his plate before everyone had taken their seats.

Just like Coen always did, he pulled Sydney's seat out for her and helped her sit down before he sat beside her at the table. He poured her a glass of wine, knowing she would need it, then poured his own. "Denise, would you like some?"

"Yeah." She practically threw her glass at him.

Coen didn't react to her utter rudeness. With a smile on his face, he poured the wine and returned the glass to her. "Anyone else?"

"Beer," Dan said.

"I apologize," Coen said. "We don't have any."

Dan looked at Sydney. "You don't have beer?" His bushy eyebrows drew together and his thick mustache twitched. "You knew we were coming and you didn't get any?"

"We don't drink beer," Sydney said calmly. "We have water and wine. What would you like?" She was shocked that she kept her voice under control. It didn't betray the pure hatred she felt underneath.

"Rude," Dan said as he shoveled mashed potatoes into his mouth. No one said grace before they began. They just started to eat everything in sight. No one thanked her for the dinner or complimented her cooking. Nothing was said for a long time. She wasn't sure if she should feel grateful or just awkward.

"Baby, this is really good. You did a wonderful job," Coen said before he kissed her on the cheek.

She smiled at him. "Thank you."

"Baby?" Dan asked incredulously. "That nickname is too intimate."

"She's my fiancé," he said calmly.

"What?" he said, food falling from his mouth. He glared at Sydney. "Is that true?"

She held up her left hand. "Yes."

"I don't remember you asking for permission, bucko," he snapped.

Coen didn't react at all. In fact, his face was stoic. Sydney was shocked by how calm he was. If his family treated her like that, she would either tell them where to go or just walk out. Coen leaned back in his chair but didn't clench his fists or glare at her stepfather. "Since her father passed away, I had no one to ask."

"I am her father."

Sydney almost shattered the wine glass under her hand. He had said that to her too many times. It was appalling and untrue. He wasn't even like a father to her, just a man that made her life miserable. She refused to let that comment slide. If she was decked in the face because of it, so be it. She wanted him to hit her. Nothing would give her greater pleasure than beating the shit out of him in front of his own son. "You are *not* my father," she said, staring directly into his eyes.

Dan met her look and rage sizzled in his irises. It made his coil snap just as much as it made hers. His possessiveness and control over her was something he enjoyed exerting. Every time she defied him, it pissed him off. He leaned forward and looked at her.

Sydney waited for him to say something but he didn't. The tension picked up in the room. Johnny swirled his fork in his potatoes, his eyes watching the whole scene. Her mother glanced at them as she buttered her roll. Sydney kept her body relaxed as she waited for him to say or do something. Finally, he picked up his fork and kept eating, backing down.

Sydney was shocked. She hadn't expected that reaction at all. He didn't even yell at her or threaten to slap her. He continued to glance at her with looks of hate but that was the worst of it. When she looked at Coen, she saw the death threat in his eyes. Now she knew why Dan didn't make a move. Coen was larger than him, his arms flanked with muscles and his shoulders wide. His chest was hidden under his shirt, but the dimensions of his chest were unmistakable. Pounds of muscle covered his chest and torso, making him a formidable opponent. If she were forced to fight him, unaware that he was proficient in different practices of martial arts, she would fear him. He was younger than Dan by many years, but that just made him even more frightening. His presence was her protection against another beating. She squeezed his hand under the table, thankful that he was there.

Her mother looked at her. "How's school, Syd?"

"It's good."

"What are you learning again?"

"I want to be a marine biologist."

"What the hell is that?" Johnny asked.

"I study the life of the ocean," she said calmly.

"Waste of time," Dan muttered as he spoke with his mouth full.

Coen looked at her mother. "She just did research with Dr. Gilbert Goldstein, one of the most respected researchers in his field. She studied the salt dilution methods of great white sharks. She's very talented and intelligent. She's one of the top students in our class."

Sydney's cheeks reddened as she listened to his praise of her. She wasn't used to someone speaking of her in an admirable way. He sounded proud of her.

Her mother acted like the information meant nothing. "You should go into hair styling. They make good money." She buttered another roll and shoved it into her mouth.

Sydney was speechless. The naivety and ignorance of her family baffled her. "This is what I love to do."

"Well, it sounds boring," Johnny said.

"It's the most fascinating thing in the world," she said quickly.

He rolled his eyes. "Sounds like you're a hippie."

"I'll take that as a compliment," she said as she drank from her wine glass again. She hardly touched her food but she wasn't hungry.

Coen waited for them to ask about him, the man she was going to marry, but none of them seemed to care. "I'm also studying marine biology."

"So you are perfect together," Dan said sarcastically.

Coen drank from his glass but said nothing.

"Where am I sleeping?" Johnny blurted.

"In the entryway," Sydney said.

"You don't have another bedroom?" he asked, annoyed.

"You saw the size of this house," she said sarcastically.

Dan narrowed his eyes at her. "Don't talk to your brother like that."

"This is my house," she snapped. "I can talk to him however I want."

His eyes lit up in flames but he still didn't say anything. His hand gripped his knife.

Coen caught the look. "I'm also a personal trainer, proficient in self-defense, martial arts, and jiu-jitsu—just to let you know."

Dan glanced at him but didn't respond to his comment. "And where will we be sleeping?"

"In the living room," Sydney said.

"What?" he snapped. "As your guests, we should get the bedroom."

Sydney crossed her arms over her chest. "No. Coen and I are sleeping there."

He raised an eyebrow. "You and Coen?" He glared at Coen. "That's the most disrespectful thing I've ever heard. You have a lot of nerve."

"I live here," Coen said calmly.

"Even worse," Dan snapped. "You aren't even married. How can you defy God like that? Living together without being married?"

Sydney hated it when he spoke of religion. He had sex with her mother before they got married. The sound of the crashing headboard always woke her up. Then, he beat her until she was put in the hospital. How dare he speak of God. "You are such a hypocrite."

Dan jumped from his seat. His chair skid across the floorboards as it moved. The table shook as he slammed his fists down, livid. Coen was on his feet just as fast, his arms dangling at his sides. Even though his stance wasn't threatening, the look in his eyes was. Sydney remained in her seat, waiting for something to happen. Coen kept his word and didn't attack but she knew it took all his patience to remain in control. A part of her wished he would just break his oath to her. Dan threw his napkin on the table. "Let's hit the beach." He walked away from the table and the other two trailed behind him.

Sydney didn't want them to linger on the small beach next to her tiny shack. It was a safe haven for her. If their skin touched the water, poison would leak inside of it. They left their plates on the table, not offering to help her clean up. She still waited in vain for a thank you.

Coen helped clean up the table. He carried the dishes to the sink and started to rinse them. She watched him for a long time, admiring his devotion to her. He was insulted and challenged but he took it passively. She knew he was strong and had a short temper. The fact he was so calm was truly astounding. She hoped he wouldn't leave her. She helped him clean the rest of the dishes and store the leftovers in Tupperware. When they were finished, Coen kissed her on the forehead. "Thank you for cooking Thanksgiving dinner."

She felt the tears in her eyes. "You're welcome."

15

The three of them stayed on the beach until the sun set over the horizon. While they were gone, she and Coen prepared the air mattresses and laid them on the floor. They gathered a few pillows and blankets. Fortunately, it was never cold on the island so extra padding wasn't a concern. And Sydney didn't care how comfortable her guests were anyway.

When they came into the house, they trailed sand everywhere because they didn't rinse off with the hose in the front. Sydney was already so annoyed that she didn't bother to reprimand them. They were rude and stupid, ignorant to everyone around them.

All three of them took a shower and used up all the hot water. The bathroom was a total mess with toothpaste and toilet paper all over the place. She suspected that Johnny trashed it on purpose. She tried to ignore it. They were only there for a few days.

"Do you need anything?" Sydney asked as she walked into the living room.

Dan and her mom were lying on the air mattress. He turned on his side. "This is going to hurt my back."

"There're a ton of hotels you can stay at," she said as she walked away. When she walked into the entry way, she looked at Johnny. "Need anything?"

He just stared at her, a hungry expression in his eyes.

"Good night, then." She felt his eyes drill holes in her backside.

When she finally closed her bedroom door and locked it, she breathed a sigh of relief. She leaned against the door and closed her eyes, thankful for the separation. Coen was already sitting in bed, his head against the headboard. His chest was bare and he only wore his boxers.

"It's only for a few days," he whispered.

"I know."

"Come to bed."

She pulled one of his shirts from his drawer and put it on, sleeping in just her underwear. She crawled into bed alongside him. He took the side closest to the door, which he didn't usually do. "The door is locked."

"I know."

She pulled the covers over her shoulder and sighed to herself. "I'm sorry you have to deal with this."

"Stop that now."

She stilled at the command in his voice. "You don't deserve it."

"I mean it, Syd."

She wrapped her arms around him and held him close, trying not to cry. "Okay."

"We're a team. This is just for a few days. After they're gone, you are never going to speak to them again. This is it—the last time."

"Okay."

He kissed her on the forehead. "Now go to sleep."

"Thank you so much," she said, squeezing him. "I don't know what I would do without you."

He ran his fingers through her hair and stilled her frantic heart. He said nothing as he caressed her, running his fingers down her smooth skin and the soft locks of her hair. Not a single inch of her skin was untouched. He massaged the area between her legs and even her toes. Somehow, it made her relax enough to fall asleep, content with his hard body in her arms.

She felt the touch of cold against her neckline. It burned slightly then slithered across her skin. A snake was crawling across her, constricting around her windpipe. She dreamt she was in a jungle, running from an unseen enemy. Her heart hammered in her chest. She opened her eyes and felt her heart fall.

A hand covered her mouth while another held a knife to Coen's throat. He was still asleep, unaware of the danger lurking so close. Her eyes widened as she looked at Johnny, a maniacal gleam in his eye. He nodded to the hand with the knife, holding it against Coen, then looked at the hand over her mouth. She knew what he meant. If she screamed, he would kill Coen.

He removed his hand, and when she didn't scream, his smile widened. His hand moved under the blanket, slithering to the area between her legs. His fingers grazed her thigh. With every passing inch, she felt bile rise in her throat. She wanted Coen to wake up to save her, but at the same time, she didn't.

"Let's go outside so we don't have to be quiet," she whispered.

Coen didn't stir at the sound of her voice.

Johnny was quiet for a long time before he held the blade against her throat instead, almost drawing blood. He grabbed her arm then gently pulled her from the bed. Coen started snoring but he still didn't wake up. With the blade still held to her skin, Johnny marched her out of the room and through the front door.

Sydney felt her heart accelerate. She had spared Coen. That was all that mattered at that point. If something happened to him, she would never be able to forgive herself.

Johnny made her sit on the top stair. With the knife still held to her throat, he walked around her then kneeled before her. In the darkness, she could see the erection in his pants. His breathing was heavy with excitement. It seemed like he would come just from getting her alone. He reached his hand up her shirt and grabbed her underwear, about to pull it down. As it started to yank, Sydney made her move.

She grabbed the knife then twisted it away from her neck, slamming it against the stairs. He still didn't release the knife so she slammed his hand down again until it finally fell free. With the knife out of the way, she kicked him back, sending him to the dirt. Adrenaline coursed through her body, giving her more strength than she thought possible. He was twice her size but that didn't slow her down. She pounced on him, slamming her fists against his face. His head flew back and surprise shined in his eyes, shocked that she was able to hit him so hard. She kicked him in the nuts and he yelled, screaming at the top of his lungs, but she punched him again. When the blood dripped from his nose, she smiled. It felt so good. Just to get more satisfaction, she socked him in the nuts again. He howled loudly, rolling over on his side.

The front door opened and Dan came running out. When he saw Johnny lying in the dirt, clutching himself, he eyed Sydney with hatred. "Get away from my son, you bitch!" He marched to her, his arms swinging at his sides. Her mother watched from the doorway, not making a move to help her.

Sydney watched him approach her, her defensive stance ready. She was ready for this, wanted it to happen. The hatred shined brighter in his eyes despite the blackness of the night. If he was ever going to kill her, he was going to do it now.

Her mom was pushed out of the way as Coen sprinted down the steps. He had his jeans on but his chest was still bare. He moved past her stepfather then placed himself in front of Sydney, his entire body blocking her from sight. She wished he hadn't intervened but she could never ask him not to. That went against everything he believed in.

"Move out of my way, boy," Dan said, grabbing his arm.

Quicker than Sydney could watch, his arm jerked away, making Dan take a step back. "Don't touch her."

He ignored him. "You beat my son, I beat you," he said, trying to walk around Coen. Coen wouldn't budge. He kept his body in front of her, completely sealing her off. "Get over here!"

"He attacked me first!" she said.

"Don't lie to me," he snapped.

"I'm not. I'm not a liar." She couldn't see his face, just Coen's back, but she could imagine the sight of his features. The look was forever ingrained into her mind. Her mother rushed to Johnny and assessed his body. She seemed to be relieved he was okay as she helped him to his feet. She expected her mother to act this way, but actually seeing it knocked the wind out of her. There was never any chance that her mother would ever love her. Sydney meant nothing to her.

"If you hit him again, I won't be so merciful," Dan said, still trying to move around Coen.

"Then tell him to keep his hands off me," Sydney said.

"My boy would do no such thing."

"Then you don't know him very well."

Coen held up his hand. "Step away from my fiancé."

Dan glared at him. "If it happens again, I won't spare you either."

Coen said nothing, but Sydney knew what he was thinking. He hoped her stepfather would throw a punch. He wanted nothing more than to kick his ass.

Dan walked back in the house, following behind Johnny. They talked inside for a long time before the house returned to quiet. Coen remained in front of her. The crickets sang in the night and a few bird calls could be heard. He finally turned around when he felt it was safe.

He grabbed her face. "Are you okay?"

"I'm fine."

He looked at her body, examining every inch of her skin. "Are you sure?"

"Coen, I'm okay."

"What the fuck happened?"

She didn't want to tell him. It would make him insane. "I got a glass of water and we started to fight. One thing led to another until we wound up out here."

"Did he hit you?"

"No."

"Did you hit him?"

"Many times. I kicked him in the nuts twice."

He breathed a sigh of relief. "I hope it hurts next time he has a boner."

She felt horrible for lying to him but she didn't know if she should tell him the truth. He had a knife pressed to his throat and he didn't even know about it. What if he turned and left, leaving her all alone. She closed her eyes. She couldn't believe how selfish she was. "I lied."

"What?"

"That isn't what happened."

He waited for her to continue.

"He came into our bedroom and held a knife to your throat. If I didn't do what he said, he was going to kill you."

He stared at her for a long time, shock on his face. "We need to go to the police, Syd."

"And say what? You were asleep the entire time then my mom and Dan caught me beating him. It's just my word against his."

He ran his fingers through his hair but said nothing.

"If you want to leave, I totally understand." She looked at the dirt below her feet.

"I'm not going anywhere without you."

"This isn't fair to you."

"You are my girl. I protect you. End of story."

"I wouldn't blame you if you left."

"Shut up," he snapped.

She flinched.

"I said I'm staying. Stop trying to convince me to go."

"Okay."

"Now let's go back to bed."

"You can sleep?"

"He won't bother us again." He grabbed her hand and helped her back inside the house. Johnny was sleeping beside his parents in the living room, under the protection of his father. Sydney couldn't help rolling her eyes. Coen guided her back into the bedroom then shut the door behind them.

"He must have picked the lock," he said. He grabbed her dresser then moved it in front of the door. He grabbed an umbrella then pinned it underneath the handle, making it impossible to turn even if the lock was picked. "He won't be able to get through that."

She finally felt safe.

"Now get to bed."

She crawled under the covers then gave him room to lie down. He sat up against the headboard and ran his fingers through her hair.

"Aren't you going to sleep?" she asked.

"No."

"I can stay awake."

"I'm not sleeping until they leave."

16

The next day, Sydney and Coen took them sightseeing around the island, showing them the different beaches and attractions. Sydney wore a hat so no one would recognize her. She wasn't just embarrassed of her family—she was ashamed.

Johnny stared at her whenever his father wasn't looking, giving her a look of lust and hate mixed together. When Coen caught the look, he would make his own venom very clear. Sydney waited for Coen to strangle him but he never did.

Sydney didn't even want to go with them but she had to drive. The idea of letting Dan drive her father's Jeep was just unacceptable. And she wouldn't let Coen offer his car instead. Even though he wanted to take care of her, this wasn't his problem. She wouldn't let him sacrifice everything.

They spent the afternoon trying to get along, listening to Dan chatter about various topics like he was actually knowledgeable about anything besides beer and porn. Her mother hardly spoke, seeming indifferent and completely dull. When she was with Sydney's father, she never shut up. She talked happily as often as she would yell at her father. That relationship wasn't healthy either but at least she had a personality. Sydney wondered if her mother was just as afraid of Dan as she was. Perhaps she was too scared to admit it.

They took them on the drive to Kailua, a tourist location with famous waterfalls and fruit stands that ran on the honor system. Her family had no respect for nature.

They littered at every stop, throwing their empty soda cans on the side of the road and their trash on the grass. Sydney picked it up and threw it in the garbage. Littering was something that got under her skin. She hated it when people didn't respect the land. Instead of arguing with them about it, she just bent over and took care of it herself. Coen watched her with a saddened expression.

He never left her side. If she had to use the bathroom, he stood outside the door like a watchdog. Whenever she went into the kitchen, he followed her like a stalker. There was never a time when she was alone. After having a knife held to her throat, she appreciated the protection. She tried to hide her fear but she was still shaken up about it.

She made dinner that night, which no one seemed to be impressed by, then cleaned up the kitchen. As always, Coen thanked her for cooking. They retired on the couch and watched television. Coen's hand was on her thigh but he wasn't watching the screen, his gaze constantly rotating to her three family members.

"Tattoos are a sin," Dan said, eyeing the ink on his forearm. "Disgusting."

Coen said nothing.

"How can you date this trash?" he said to Sydney.

"I ask Mom that all the time."

"What did you say?"

"You heard me." She stood up, Coen following her immediately.

The spit flew from Dan's mouth when he spoke. "I'm tired of putting up with this disrespect. It's bullshit! Bullshit!" He slammed his arm down then pointed his finger at her face. "We came all the way here to see you on Thanksgiving and this is how you treat us, you little bitch."

"Don't pull that shit with me," she snapped. "You only came here for a free vacation. You got it so it's time to leave. Get the fuck out."

"You are about to get slapped," he threatened.

"Fuck you, you white trash piece of shit. You talk about my fiancé like that again and I'll punch you square in the mouth."

He shook his head, his cheeks turning red.

"Do it, asshole! Hit me! What's steadied your hand? Is it because I have a real man here that could beat you senseless with one arm, you fucking pussy?"

He became even angrier. Coen stood by her side, his arms tense. He waited for the right moment.

"Stop!"

They all turned to see her mom standing there, arms raised.

"Stop fighting," she continued. "This has gone on long enough."

Sydney was so shocked, her mouth dropped.

Dan turned, his ferocity directed at her. "Shut your mouth!"

"Please stop yelling at my daughter."

Suddenly, Dan marched away from her and reached his bag. Sydney wasn't sure what he was doing. It looked like he was leaving. She hoped he was.

"Don't go," her mother begged. "I'm sorry."

When Dan stood up, he was holding a bat in his hands. Sydney felt her heart fall. Her stepfather raised the bat then aimed it for her mother's head. She was so shocked, she couldn't react. Her mouth was open but there were no words. He swung it at her mother but it never reached its mark.

Coen stepped in, getting in front of her mother just in time. The bat broke in half as it smashed into his chest, pieces of it flying through the air. He fell to the ground, his eyes closed and his hand over his chest. Her mother looked down at him, her hands covering her mouth.

Dan raised his boot to kick him.

Sydney charged him then pushed him away, sending him against the wall. Every move Coen taught her came back to her. She punched him in the nose then the chin and threw him on the ground. When Johnny came to his aid, she kicked him in the nuts, sending him to the ground.

"Don't you touch my fiancé like that!" She punched Dan in the face again.

He scrambled to his feet then wiped the blood away. "I don't need this!" He grabbed his bag then looked at Johnny. "Let's go."

Johnny finally rose to his feet, still cupping his balls, then grabbed his belongings. He stumbled behind his father as they headed to the front door.

Sydney rushed to Coen then lifted up his shirt, seeing a bruise form on his chest. The purple color told her how painful it was. Luckily, his sternum wasn't broken and his ribs seemed to be intact. His muscled chest took most of the pain. Tears fell from her eyes as she looked at him. "Babe, are you okay?"

He nodded, his eyes still closed. "I'm fine. Just get rid of them."

"Do you need to go to the hospital?"

"No," he said through clenched teeth, fighting the pain. "I'll be fine. Get rid of them."

Dan came back into the room. He looked at her mother. "Come on!" His hands clenched at his sides, staring her down. Her green eyes lost their light as she looked at him. There was fear deep in their abyss. "I said come on."

Sydney looked at her mother. "Stay here, Mom. You don't have to go."

She said nothing.

"We'll go to the police and tell them everything that happened. They'll go to jail and we'll never have to see them again."

She still stared at Dan.

Sydney reached for her hand, tears streaming down her face. "Mom, please. Don't go to him. I can help you."

"GET YOUR ASS OVER HERE!"

Her mom pulled her hand away.

"No!" Sydney yelled. "Don't do this! He's just going to keep hurting you. I can get you out."

Her mom averted her gaze then grabbed her belongings, walking over to him. When she reached him, he slapped her across the face. "Good girl."

Sydney jumped to her feet, dashing toward him with the intent of murder.

Her mom stepped in front of her, one hand covering her swollen cheek. She said nothing as she stared at Sydney, tears glistening in her eyes. Without saying another word, she turned around and followed Dan like an obedient dog, catching a cab back to the airport.

Sydney was glued to the floor, unable to move. Her mother went back to Dan—voluntarily. She had a way out but she didn't want it. She wanted to stay with him. The tears kept pouring down as Sydney replayed all the events in her head. When she remembered Coen, lying on the floorboard, she went back to him with a pillow in hand. She tucked it under his head.

"I'm sorry," she said as she kissed his cheeks. "I'm so sorry about this."

"Baby, calm down."

"We need to take you to the hospital."

"It's just a bruise."

"You could have internal bleeding."

"I don't."

"Are you a doctor?"

He placed her hand over his chest, staying away from the bruise. "Breathe with me."

She swallowed her tears and did as he asked, following the relaxed pace of his expanding lungs. Within a minute, she felt calm.

Coen sat up with a groan then looked at her, checking her arms and neck. "Are you okay?"

She nodded.

"They are gone. You never have to see them again."

Her lips trembled, the emotion taking over. "She wanted to go."

His eyes sagged in despair. "I know."

"Why?"

He said nothing for a long time. "Not everyone is as strong as you."

"He'll kill her."

He sighed. "There's nothing you can do for her. You gave her a way out but she didn't take it. You can't help someone who doesn't want to be helped."

She cried. "Should I tell the police?"

"I hate to say this, but it might get her in deeper. When they don't have enough evidence to bring a case against Dan, he'll probably hurt her even more."

"Then what do I do?"

"Nothing, Syd. You already did everything you could."

"I can't believe you took that hit for her. You didn't have to do that."

He ran his fingers through her hair. "She's a lady and she's still your mother. I wouldn't let anything happen to her."

She wiped her tears away. "I'm so sorry."

"I would do it again in a heartbeat—anything to spare you pain."

"I don't deserve you."

"That's completely untrue."

She collapsed in his arms, crying to herself. "I'm so glad I have you."

He kissed her forehead. "And I'm happy I have you."

She closed her eyes and said nothing. All the drama that happened the past few days left her heart feeling black and frozen. She was glad she never told anyone about her family or where she came from. It was disturbing and embarrassing. Coen was the only person who really knew her like no one else. She also knew he was the first person to truly love her. He was such an amazing man and she didn't know what she had done to deserve him. She counted her blessings. Not only was she alive, but her past was finally behind her. She had her new family now.

17

"Baby, I'm fine."

She grabbed his shoulders and kept him pinned to the bed. "Just rest, okay?" The tears sprang from her eyes every time she looked at the huge mark covering his chest. It was a deeper shade of black and blue when they woke up the next morning.

"I'm fine—really," he said as he looked at her.

"I'm so sorry," she said for the hundredth time as tears ran down her face. She kissed his chest lightly. "I'm so sorry." The ugly bruise was entirely her fault. It killed her to see him in so much pain. It was unacceptable. "I'll get you some lunch. Please just stay there."

He grabbed her arm and steadied it. "I'm going to be okay."

She shook her head. "No, you won't."

He looked into her face. "I'm not a liar, Syd. It doesn't hurt."

"Yes, it does."

He sighed. "It doesn't hurt as much as it did yesterday. I don't need to stay in bed. I don't have the flu."

"You still need to rest."

"We rested all last night and this morning. I'm okay now."

She took a deep breath. "I'm sorry. This is just so hard to see."

He was quiet for a moment before he rose from the bed then grabbed a shirt from his drawer. He put it on so the horrific bruise wouldn't be visible anymore. He returned to the bed and sat down. She pulled back the covers and waited for him to get in.

He shook his head. "I don't need to lie down."

"Please, Coen."

The desperation in her eyes made him climb on the bed and move under the covers. "It's just a bruise. It will heal and disappear like all the others."

"The bat broke in half when it hit you."

"What can I say? I'm like a concrete wall," he said with a smile.

She didn't laugh or hide the frown on her face.

"Please stop worrying," he said with a sigh. "If anything, this is hurting me."

"You shouldn't have to deal with this."

He looked at her, straight in the eye. "I would have taken a lot worse if I had to. This is nothing, Syd."

She shook her head. "You shouldn't have to."

He grabbed her hand. "It's over—they're gone. Let's just move on. Stop beating yourself up for what happened to me."

She placed her fingers over his chest and glided them across the shirt, trying to make him relax. He leaned back on the pillow and ran his fingers through her hair, trying to dispel the tears on her face. She seemed to calm down after he covered himself with a shirt. The sight was too much for her.

He sat up to move out of bed but she pushed him back by the arms. "No."

He glared at her. "I'm not staying on bed rest forever." He sat up again but she pushed him back.

She pulled down the blankets then kneeled between his legs. As soon as he realized what she was doing, he stopped.

She grabbed the rim of his boxers and pulled them off, revealing his limp cock. After she tossed his underwear on the ground, it sprang to life, knowing exactly what was going to happen. His breath caught in his throat as he watched her. He wasn't trying to get out of bed anymore. Sydney grabbed her shirt and pulled it from her body then unclasped her bra. Coen's breathing only increased as he watched her.

"You don't have to do this," he said weakly. His voice was so quiet she almost didn't hear him.

She bent down and licked the tip, making him gasp so loud it was almost a scream. She pulled away and looked into his face. "You want me to stop?"

He stared at her for a while before he finally shook his head, embarrassment flooding his cheeks.

Sydney leaned back over him. Before her lips pressed against him, he tensed up, anticipating the wetness of her mouth. She felt guilty because they hadn't fooled around in days. The sexual frustration oozed out of him. He never said anything but she knew he was horny as hell.

When her lips surrounded him, he gasped again, breathing like he just ran a marathon. His hand immediately fisted her hair and his hips started to rock into her gently. His cock felt harder than it ever had as she swirled her tongue around the tip then down the shaft. Every time she took him entirely down her throat, he shook. Her hair was sprawled across his stomach and hips, and he fisted it gently. She knew he loved her hair, the color and the texture. People thought she styled it to have that beach wave to it, but she never did anything. It was natural.

When his hips started to convulse, she knew she was on the verge of having an orgasm. They had just begun and he already met his threshold. That didn't surprise her since their sex life had been dormant for so long. She pulled him out of her mouth then rubbed her chest against him, pressing her tits together.

Coen bit his lip while he watched her. His free hand clenched the bed sheets, trying to process all the pleasure circulating in his veins.

She returned her lips to him and shoved him to the back of her throat, knowing he was going to come any second. His breathing was deep and raspy, forced from his lips against his restraint. He laid his head back and closed his eyes. When his dick twitched, she knew the moment had arrived. He moaned loudly, gently thrusting himself inside of her as he shot out with a rapid explosion. She continued to go down on him as he released, waiting until he was completely finished before she pulled away.

He ran his hands through his hair and kept his eyes closed, his chest still rising and falling rapidly. He was a broken mess, pieces shattered across the bed. His explosion had sucked the life force out of him. Now he just tried to come down from his high. She crawled off of him then pulled the blankets back up, tucking him in.

"Bed rest," she said firmly.

He opened his eyes and looked at her. "That felt so good."

"Well, I've had a lot of practice."

He smiled at her. "I'm sorry I couldn't last longer."

She kissed him on the forehead. "It's okay. I know I haven't been satisfying you lately."

"Don't apologize," he said quickly.

"I'll make it up to you." She glanced at his chest then back at him.

"You don't owe me anything, baby."

She ran her fingers through his hair. "Get some sleep."

"That's all I've been doing."

"Get more of it."

"Let's take a shower. There's something I want to show you."

She raised an eyebrow. "What?"

"You'll see."

"Well, it will have to wait. You need to rest."

He rolled his eyes. "I'm fine."

"If you want another blow job, you are staying right here."

He growled. "Well, I'll have to miss out then. Come on. Let's take a shower."

"I want you to get better," she said as she touched his hand.

"Baby, I am better. Now let's go."

She sighed. "Okay."

"And I still expect that blow job."

She rubbed her nose against his. "I'll give you as many as you want."

"Can I get that in writing?"

She laughed. "My word isn't good enough?"

"You're a woman—of course not."

"Well, you'll just have to trust me."

"I will." He pulled the blankets back then rose to his feet. "Let's take a shower."

"Where are we going?"

"You'll see when we get there."

They both showered and got ready. Coen pulled out an outfit and told her to wear it. Normally she wore shorts and a small top, but he wanted her to wear jeans and a nice blouse. She assumed they were going to a nice dinner. She did as he asked and put it on. Coen wore black slacks and a collared shirt. He looked handsome like he always did. He wrapped a tie around his neck then fixed it.

"You look so sexy," she said as she wrapped her arms around his waist.

"Thank you," he said as he rubbed his nose against hers. "But I don't compete with you." He kissed her on the forehead then walked to the front door. "Let's go."

She followed him out the door then into the car. He started the engine and they pulled onto the dirt road. They didn't head to the coast where all the shopping and restaurants were. Instead, he drove further into the island, away from the tourist spots. She wasn't sure where they were going. When he pulled onto a street in a nice neighborhood, two story houses with large yards, she was even more confused.

"Where are we going?"

He pulled over and parked in front of a large white house. There were two wreaths on the door and Christmas lights decorated the outside. A large tree stood in the front yard, stretching high into the sky. It was on a slight rise and the mountains could be seen in the background.

"What is this?" she asked.

"My parents' house."

She looked at him. "Why are we here?"

"To celebrate Thanksgiving."

"But that was days ago."

"Yeah, my parents decided to have it today instead."

"Why?"

"So you could join us."

She felt her heart flutter. "What? You asked them to do that?"

He smiled. "No. They offered. They want you to be here."

"Did you tell them about…"

"Yes. But I left the major things out. They want you to spend the holiday with us, Syd. They are excited to meet you."

She looked out the window and stared at the house. She saw people inside, drinking from their wine glasses as they stood around the tree. Tears formed under her eyes. "I don't know what to say."

"Let's just go inside."

"I can't believe you did this for me."

"My family already loves you, Syd. I didn't do this—they did."

"Why?"

"They know I'm madly in love with you."

"They still want me here even after you told them about my family?"

He ran his fingers through her hair. "They love you even more, baby."

A tear fell from her eye and she wiped it away. "That's so sweet of them."

"Now let's go get our grub on," he said as he opened the door. He helped her down then walked her to the front door, holding her hand.

"Wait." She grabbed the engagement ring to take it off.

"No," he said, steadying her hand. "Leave it."

"But they'll see it."

"Don't worry about it. Just leave it."

She left the ring on her finger, unsure how this was going to work. If his family saw her wear his grandmother's ring, wouldn't they ask questions or assume they were really engaged? "I hope they like me," she blurted.

"They will. It's impossible not to." He walked to the door then knocked on it. The sound of merry voices could be heard from the outside. A high-pitched laughter was infectious enough to make Sydney smile. She tried to recall a time when her mother laughed after she remarried. She couldn't think of a single instance.

A tall brunette opened the door, smiling at them brightly. Her hair was short, not even reaching her ears, but she looked elegant and beautiful. Her eyes were blue just like Coen's. There was no doubt that this was his mother. The woman glanced at Coen but her eyes were focused on Sydney.

"Sydney!" she said in delight. She walked through the door and wrapped her arms around Sydney, holding her tightly. "I'm so glad you're here. Thank you for coming."

Sydney returned her embrace, warmth radiating from her body. "Thank you for having me."

She pulled away. "And you're so beautiful. Coen never lies."

She blushed. "Thank you."

"Come, come," she said as she grabbed her hand and led her inside.

When they walked through the door, other family members rose from their seats and approached them. A middle aged man smiled at Sydney then hugged her as well. Judging by his chiseled jaw and height, he was Coen's father.

"I'm Nathan," he said as he pulled away. "I'm very delighted to meet you."

"It's nice to meet you too," she said politely.

"And I'm Vivian," his mother said quickly. "Sorry. I forgot to mention that."

"It's okay," Sydney said with a smile.

"And I'm Coen's younger, but much more attractive brother," a guy said as he hugged her. She was startled by the touch. Every person hugged her. No one shook her hand. The affection was welcome, but unexpected. "So, let me know if you want to upgrade."

She laughed. "I'm very happy with what I have."

Coen wrapped his arm around her waist. "Sorry, bro. She doesn't have a sister."

"Damn," he said.

"His name is Jordan," Coen added. He turned to an older couple. She assumed they were his grandparents. "This is my maternal grandmother, Lori, and my grandfather, Jeremy." They both hugged her, making Sydney feel cherished.

"Stacy!"

She looked up and saw his uncle.

"I'm just kidding, Sydney." He hugged her too. "Thanks for coming."

"Thank you, Dr. Goldstein."

"Call me Gilbert."

Vivian clapped her hands together. "Dinner is ready. I hope your stomachs are empty."

"I'm starving," Sydney blurted.

Coen looked at his mother. "This one can eat more than I can."

"Good," she said. "I cooked way too much."

They walked into the dining area, which had a dark wooden table with a red table cloth. Most of the food was already sitting on the surface. They had gold silverware and matching napkins. Coen pulled out her chair and helped her sit down. When she glanced up, all the family members smiled at Coen, obviously impressed by his manners. When he sat beside her, he rested his hand on her thigh.

Lori passed the stuffing to Sydney. "So you are studying marine biology like Coen?" she asked.

"Yes," Sydney answered. "It's definitely my passion."

"She's one of the smartest undergraduates I've ever had," his uncle said as he scooped the cranberry sauce onto his turkey.

Sydney's cheeks turned red.

"She gets a perfect score on every test," Coen said with a smile.

His grandfather laughed. "That must be convenient to cheat off your girlfriend."

Coen laughed. "It's definitely a plus."

"His grade did skyrocket after he started talking to Sydney," his father said.

"Well, at least you know they were actually studying," Dr. Goldstein said with a laugh.

Sydney laughed, overcome by the merriment.

His mother looked at her. "What do you want to pursue?"

"I was hoping to get my PhD."

"Another crazy," his uncle said as he took a bite.

Sydney laughed. "I know Coen wouldn't disagree."

He shrugged. "I'm just with you because of your looks."

"Do you want to teach at a university?' his mother asked.

"Yes. And do research," Sydney said. She ate her vegetables and rolls and loved the taste. No one made a comment about her eating choice. She didn't reach for the ham or the turkey but no one seemed to notice. Usually, she was berated for being a vegetarian.

His family joked with each other and discussed their lives. His grandparents were retired from the post office. That's where they met fifty years ago. His father worked in construction and just got a contract for a new hotel on the other side of the island. His mother was a housewife. When she remembered that Coen's parents almost got divorced, she found that hard to believe. They seemed so happy. No one mentioned his sister who passed away. She did notice pictures of her everywhere, however. It made her happy to know that they didn't give into the depression of their past, but decided to be merry while always remembering her.

Sydney ate more than she should. By the time she was done, her stomach started to cramp. Thankfully, her shirt was a little loose to hide her bulging stomach. Coen ate two servings of food because he was a garbage disposal like that. When he coughed on his food, he touched his chest. He tried to act like everything was fine but she knew he was in serious pain. The bat broke in half when it collided with this chest. How could he not be in agonizing pain? Every time she thought of it, she realized she wasn't good enough for him. His family was nothing but respectful toward her. In fact, they treated her like she was already family. She never felt more loved in her life, like she belonged somewhere. It was enough to bring tears to her eyes, but she held them back.

"Now we say what we're thankful for," his mother said from the head of the table. Sydney assumed this was a tradition because no one questioned her words. "I'm thankful for having such a wonderful and beautiful family." She turned to Sydney. "And having one more." Sydney smiled, unsure what to say.

His father wiped his mouth with a napkin. "I'm thankful that I don't have to do the dishes."

Everyone laughed and Vivian narrowed her eyes at him playfully.

"What are you thankful for, Jordan?" his mother asked.

"The beautiful beach." His mother smiled. "There are so many hot chicks down there."

His grandpa laughed and clapped him on the shoulder. "That's why I'm there every day."

Vivian rolled her eyes. "My boys are something else."

His grandpa nodded. "I'm thankful for the same thing."

Lori hit him playfully. "Don't be an old pervert."

"Too late."

"I know where I get it from," Jordan said with a laugh.

Lori shook her head. "Well, I'm thankful for the beautiful sunrise that I see every morning from my bedroom window."

Jordan rolled his eyes. "That's boring, Grandma."

Vivian looked at Gilbert. "And what are you thankful for, Brother?"

He thought for a moment before he spoke. "For all the living things in this world. There is more beauty in a single shell than all the skyscrapers of this country."

Sydney nodded, understanding his meaning.

Coen looked at his family. "I'm thankful for the beautiful woman in my life." He leaned in and kissed her on the cheek. "For having her love." His brother rolled his eyes and his grandmother made an awe sound. "And I'm thankful I'm passing my classes this semester."

His mother laughed. "I'm glad our money isn't being wasted." She looked at Sydney. "And what are you thankful for, dear?"

She twisted her hands in her lap, feeling suddenly nervous. "For the best Thanksgiving I've ever had."

Vivian's eyes softened when she listened to her. Even Jordan seemed touched by her words. Coen looked at her.

"This is my best Thanksgiving too."

"Really?"

He nodded.

Vivian rose from her seat. "It's time to get the dishes started."

All the men flew from their chairs and dashed to the living room.

Sydney laughed even though she knew she shouldn't. Only Coen remained behind. They both gathered the plates and helped his mother clean the dishes, stuffing them into the dishwasher and covering the leftover food for days to come. When they were finished, they went into the living room and played board games. Everyone was involved and no one refused to sit out. Coen's family was competitive but not in an aggressive way. When Sydney won every game, they all seemed truly impressed.

"Syd's a genius," Coen explained.

His grandpa pointed at her. "Keep her around, boy. She'll be great to have for bingo at the senior citizen hall."

He laughed. "Thanks for the advice."

When they were tired of playing board games, they sat on the couch and ate cookies and pie, drinking an assortment of wine. The television was on so everyone watched it. Sydney curled up next to Coen and leaned against his body. She wasn't uncomfortable being affectionate in front of his family. She felt like she was already a member of it.

When it got late, everyone said their goodbyes. His mother hugged Sydney tightly then kissed her on the cheek. "Thank you so much for coming."

"Thank you for having me. Everything was great."

"You're very welcome, dear."

Jordan hugged her. "Let me know if you have any cute friends that like younger guys."

She laughed. "I'll see what I can do."

Coen waved to everyone then walked Sydney to the car, opening the door for her. When they pulled away from the house, she stared at it until it was no longer in sight. That was the best holiday she ever had, other than the ones she spent alone at the shack. His family was so sweet and amazing, treating her like they loved her. When her family came, they treated Coen like he was garbage on the street. The memory of their visit still hung heavy on her heart. Coen had put up with so much bullshit for her. It was unbelievable. She didn't feel worthy of him. In fact, she didn't deserve him at all. She had nothing to offer him except baggage and emotional problems for years to come.

They were silent on the drive home. Sydney felt the tears bubble under her eyes when she realized what she had to do. She wasn't being fair to Coen. He deserved something more than her. When he parked the car, she didn't even realize they were home, her mind elsewhere. When they got out and walked back the house, she stopped before they reached the steps.

"Thank you for taking me to your Thanksgiving," she said quietly.

"Thank you for coming."

A tear fell down her cheek. "I can't do this anymore, Coen."

He stared at her, saying nothing for a long time. His eyes lingered on the tear sticking to her cheek until it dripped from her chin. "What does that mean?"

"I want to break up."

"What?" he asked, confused.

She took a deep breath. "You don't deserve this, Coen, to settle for someone who can't offer you anything. My family is nothing but an embarrassment. They treated you like you were a dog, giving you no respect whatsoever. Your family was so sweet to me, treating me like I was one of their own. I don't come from a good place. I come from garbage. You deserve someone so much better than me. I can't do this anymore."

He stepped closer to her. "Syd, we aren't breaking up."

"Yes, we are."

"I love you because of who you are, not where you come from. Your past doesn't mean anything to me. So what if your mother is weak and pathetic, your stepfather deserves the electric chair, and your stepbrother is someone I would love to kill with my bare hands? They aren't you, Syd. I love you for you, not because of your family."

"But I'm—"

"I don't love you in spite of your past. I love you because of it. You are strong, Syd. You got out and moved here, making a life for yourself. You chose your own fate when you took defense classes, empowering yourself to never be the victim again. You are truly exceptional, inspiring. You are selfless and loyal, putting other's

173

happiness before your own. You are insanely brilliant, putting your abilities to good use. You are so much more than I'll ever be. I don't deserve you, baby. It's not the other way around. Don't ever use your family as an excuse to keep me away. It won't work."

She looked down at the ground, still avoiding his gaze. His words meant the world to her, but she was so ashamed of her life experiences. He had taken a bat to the chest, something that could have killed him. How could she let him stay with her after that? She lifted her left hand and grabbed the engagement ring.

He saw her movement. "Don't."

"I can keep this."

"I said don't."

She pulled it off and offered it to him. "Find someone who deserves to wear this."

"You are the only person I would ever give this to."

She kept her hand held out, waiting for him to take it. He didn't move.

Coen lowered himself to one knee. "Sydney, I love you for you, no other reason. I would be honored if you spent the rest of your life with me. Please put that back on and marry me."

She stared at him, unable to process his words. He just proposed to her, something she never expected. "Please don't do this."

"Do what?"

"You don't need to ask me to marry you to convince me you want to be with me. I could never be your wife. You deserve someone so much better. I know you gave this to me as an act. Please don't feel bad for taking it back. I understand, Coen."

"I don't want it," he said firmly.

"Coen, stop making this hard for me. We shouldn't be together. I understand that. Now take it."

"No. I want you to have it."

"Please don't do this to me."

"What?"

"Try to prove that you want to be with me. Just take it and leave."

He rose to his feet then looked at her. He glanced at the ring then back to her face. She waited for him to take it but he didn't reach for it. Instead, he just stared at her. His eyes shined a brighter shade of blue as he looked at her. He was the most handsome man she had ever seen. She couldn't imagine her life without him, but she couldn't let him settle for her either.

"Seahorse, look at the inner band."

Her hand shook. "What?"

He nodded. "Look."

She stared at him for a long time before she pulled the ring back. She looked at him one more time but she turned the ring, seeing the engraving inside the metal.

My Seahorse

She gasped, covering her mouth.

"I had that engraved before I gave it to you. I knew when I asked you to put on that ring I wasn't going to want you to take it off ever. There was nothing you could do or say to change my feelings for you. I wanted you for the rest of my life. I still feel that way."

She finally looked at him, tears streaming down her face.

"Your family changed nothing. My feelings are as eternal as that metal. They will never dull or decay. My entire family knows we're engaged, but I told them you were too upset about your family's visit to celebrate it or acknowledge it. There isn't a doubt in my mind that you'll say yes."

He grabbed her hand then kneeled down again. "Now marry me."

She smiled at him, unable to control the joy she felt.

He grabbed the ring and returned it to her finger.

"Yes," she whispered. "Yes."

He rose to his feet then wrapped his arms around her, holding her to his chest. "Thank you for being my seahorse."

She held him tightly, saying nothing.

He pulled away and kissed her forehead. "Are you going to stop being stupid now?"

"I—I just don't deserve you."

He sighed. "So that's a no?"

She smiled. "I'm so happy I get to spend the rest of my life with you."

"That's better," he said with a smile. "And we don't have to get married right away. I know we haven't been together very long. What if we did it right after graduation? Until then, I could move in with you."

"That sounds perfect."

"Good."

"Coen?"

"Baby?"

"I love you so much."
"I love you too."

Epilogue

Sydney's friends were both surprised and happy by their serious engagement. They got together and helped Coen move his belongings to the shack. Sydney had the hardest time telling Henry. He already accepted her relationship to Coen, but marriage was very serious.

"Congratulations," he said as he hugged her.

"Thank you."

He pulled away. The light was absent in his eyes. The depth of his irises was as dark as underground caves. The smile on his face was convincing, but not the look in his eyes. He looked broken, lost in despair.

"I'm so sorry," she whispered.

"There's no reason to be sorry, Syd. I'm very happy for you. I mean it."

She nodded. "I love you."

"I know."

She hugged him again. "It's going to be okay."

"I'm fine, Syd. Don't worry about me." He pulled away. "I'm going to finish unloading the truck." He turned around and joined everyone else, carrying boxes and bags into the house.

Coen came to her and stood beside her, watching their friends carry everything into the house like working ants. "How'd it go?"

"He said he's happy for us."

"I'm glad we didn't have to keep it a secret this time," he said with a smile.

She didn't laugh.

"He'll be okay, baby."

"I just wish things were diffcrent."

"He'll move on in his own time."

"I hate causing him pain."

"It's not your fault that everyone falls in love with you."

"Not everyone."

"My brother has a crush on you."

"Well, that's just weird."

"My brother is weird."

She laughed. "At least he likes me."

"My whole family likes you."

She stared at the house and watched her friends load everything through the door. Coen didn't have a lot of stuff, but he still needed help moving everything. With the extra help, they were happy to get everything in a single trip. She was excited to live with him, knowing he would be there every night when she went to bed. "Two years is a long time."

He looked at her. "What do you mean?"

"It's just so far away."

He smiled at her. "What are you suggesting?"

"If we are already living together, why don't we just get married now?"

"I like that idea."

"When?"

"When school is out."

"Let's do it."

"Really? It's not too soon?"

"If we got married the day we met, it still wouldn't be too soon."

"So, we are doing this?"

He grabbed her face and kissed her. "Let's start planning. The sooner I'm your husband, the happier I'll be."

"The sooner I'm your seahorse, the happier I'll be."

"A marriage license is just a piece of paper. You already are my seahorse, baby." He looked into her green eyes, not just seeing the entire world like he usually did. He saw every holiday with his family, his son and his daughter, their first fight, the first time they slept apart, their family vacations, everything—his whole world.

Sydney knew what he was thinking when he stared at her. Her thoughts were the same. He was everything to her, a new beginning. The past was something that would haunt her forever, but it seemed to disappear when she was with him, numbing the pain of her heart. She didn't realize how broken she was until he put her back together. His love was the glue of her frame. She wasn't the same person she used to be. She came out the other side stronger than she had ever been. Coen was the man who would make her stronger, complementing her strengths and her weaknesses. Perhaps they weren't soul mates, but they chose each other out of all the other fish in the sea. His arm linked around hers, acting as the tail that held her to his chest. She intertwined hers around his, chaining together. They stared at each other for a long time, holding each other. Sydney knew they would never let go.

The story continues....

Connected By the Tide

Henry and Renee

(Book Three in the Hawaiian Crush Series)

Available Now

About the Author

E. L. Todd was raised in California where she attended California State University, Stanislaus and received her bachelor's degree in biological sciences, then continued onto her master's degree in education. While she considers science to be interesting, her true passion is writing. She is also the author of the *Soul Saga Trilogy, The Alpha Series, and her bestselling novel, Only For You, the first installment of the Forever and Always Series.* She is also an assistant editor at Final-Edits.com.

By E. L. Todd

Soul Catcher

(Book One of the Soul Saga)

Soul Binder

(Book Two of the Soul Saga)

Soul Relenter

(Book Three of the Soul Saga)

Only For You

(Book One of the Forever and Always Series)

Forever and Always

(Book Two of the Forever and Always Series)

Edge of Love

Connected by the Sea

(Book One of the Hawaiian Crush Series)

Breaking Through the Waves

(Book Two of the Hawaiian Crush Series)

Connected by the Tide

(Book Three of the Hawaiian Crush Series)

Taking the Plunge

(Book Four of the Hawaiian Crush Series)

Made in the USA
Columbia, SC
27 May 2021